A BEACH BUM BOOKS MURDER MYSTERY

I0769730

Published by Beach Bum Books. First edition, 2025.

Beach Bum Books is an imprint of Gordon Publishing Collective and a proud supporter of Save the Manatee Club, an award-winning national nonprofit and membership-based organization established in 1981 by the late renowned singer-songwriter, author, and entrepreneur Jimmy Buffett and former U.S. Senator Bob Graham when we was governor of Florida. Save the Manatee Club's mission is to protect manatees and their aquatic habitat. A portion of proceeds from all Beach Bum Books sales are donated to the organization.

www.BeachBumBooks.com
www.GordonPublishingCo.com
info@GordonPublishingCo.com

ISBN: 979-8-9913656-7-3

Frenchman
for
the
Night

*For my mother, who inspired both my love of
Jimmy Buffett and of murder mysteries*

CHAPTER 1
ISLAND SHADOWS

The Green Parrot hummed the way only a Key West bar could hum on an early October evening—alive with sweat, rumors, and half-finished decorations. A string of skeletons tangled with faded Mardi Gras beads hung from the rafters. A papier-mâché mermaid in a pirate hat leaned precariously over the stage, and someone had taped a "Sexy Frankenstein Wanted" flyer on the jukebox.

The rain had come and gone by four. The sidewalk was still damp, heat rising from the concrete in a slow shimmer. Inside, the fans spun half-heartedly overhead, pushing the muggy air in circles. The air conditioning was on, but it seemed to have to work overtime to beat back the humid air as hurricane season was nearing an end. Behind the bar, Pati wiped down the wood with long, deliberate strokes, as if she could smooth out more than just condensation rings. She didn't mind the early shift. Locals came out before the sun dipped too far and the humidity got drunk on itself. The tourists rolled in later, drunk already or soon to be.

"Found her like a seashell offering," Big Tom was saying, too loud, to no one in particular. "Laid out all proper—arms crossed, head tilted like she was whisperin' secrets to the moon."

Pati didn't look up. She recognized the cadence. Tom was on his second beer and his third retelling.

"Islamorada," he added. "Two nights ago. No ID. Just that look on her face."

At the far end of the bar, two regulars sat. Casey let her pencil still mid-sketch. She and Phillip were seated side by side, drinks sweating beside them. Casey's sketchpad was open to what looked like a rough study of the bartender herself—Pati's brows narrowed in playful suspicion, caught mid-shake of a cocktail tin.

"She had blue eyes," Tom said. "Young. Pretty. I saw a photo. Sorta eerie, the way she was laid out. Like a valentine someone forgot to send."

"Jesus, Tom," someone muttered. "Tone it down. You're creeping out the tourists."

A pair of sunburnt Midwesterners clutching daiquiris glanced over nervously.

Pati tossed a bar rag at Tom's arm. "You're gonna scare off the tip money."

Tom raised his hands, grinning. "Just sayin' what I heard. Sheriff's deputy is my niece's ex. Said it looked staged."

Phillip glanced at him, face unreadable, and took a quiet sip of his beer. Then, as if weighing a memory, he said, "That kind of positioning... I've seen it before. In parts of Corsica. Mourning rites. You pose the body so the soul doesn't forget the way home."

Casey blinked. "That's… grim."

Phillip shrugged one shoulder. "It's meant to be respectful."

"And creepy," Casey added, turning back to her sketch. "Respectfully creepy."

Pati cracked a smile but didn't laugh. There was something about this story that settled wrong. It wasn't that it was unusual—it wasn't. The Keys had always been a strange place. But something in the detail—a body placed like an offering, blue eyes wide open, no ID—stuck with her. And Tom's theatrical telling only made it worse, even if he was mostly full of bullshit.

She'd seen enough to know when something wasn't just a bad night gone wrong. And she'd seen a bad night gone wrong once or twice before. Wasn't it just a few months ago Casey got pissed and ran out into that storm? Pati thought. Thank god, Phillip went after her. She could've ended up like that poor girl on Islamorada.

Pati thought back to that night. She barely knew Phillip then. Just that he was quiet, an artist from Southernmost Tattoo, and he had a French accent. He's come out of his shell since meeting Casey, and Pati liked to see that.

The door creaked open before she could dwell on her regulars any further. It let in a slice of early-evening sunlight, the kind that made the bar look older than it was—every scratch in the floorboards, every crack in the baseboard shadows came into sharper view. And in that light stood a man, just slightly too stiff to belong.

He wore a pale button-down tucked into dark slacks. Real shoes, not sandals. Hair neatly combed, face calm. No one dressed like that this time of year unless they were either on the wrong vacation or from somewhere colder.

"Bonsoir," he said, stepping forward.

Pati raised a brow. "Hey there."

"I was told this was the best place for something to drink."

"By who, the ghosts?" Pati chuckled.

He smiled faintly. "Perhaps."

She sized him up, her eyebrow arching. "You want something weird, don't you?"

"Wine, if it's not too much trouble. Red, a beaujolais if you have it."

"Hm," she replied, reaching for the half-open bottle of beaujolais. Pati poured the glass. "Not as weird as I thought."

He accepted it delicately, with a small nod. "Merci."

"So, where you from…" Pati trailed off, leaving room for the new customer to fill in his name.

"Michel," he said. "From Quebec City."

She slid him the glass. He sipped. Outside, the sun dipped just low enough to make the shadows look longer than they should.

"That explains the accent," Pati smiled. Maybe he is just awkward, she thought.

Michel didn't take a seat right away. Instead, he stood at the bar with his wine glass, letting his eyes drift around the room like he was trying to memorize it—every crooked sign, every worn barstool, every face.

Pati clocked it all.

He wasn't doing the usual tourist thing—no phone out, no questions about the specials, no gawking at the wall of concert posters. He looked like he belonged in a museum lobby, not in a bar where a plastic skeleton was currently humping a rubber chicken in a pirate hat.

"You just get in?" she asked, wiping her hands on a towel.

"Earlier this week." He smiled, that quiet, precise smile. "I've rented a small place down by White Street. Very charming."

Before she could reply, Michel drifted a few stools down, toward Casey and Phillip.

"May I?" he asked, gesturing to the empty seat beside them.

Phillip gave a noncommittal nod. Casey smiled politely, more out of habit than invitation.

Michel set down his glass and nodded toward Casey's sketchpad. "That's a lovely hand. Confident line work. May I ask what you're drawing?"

Casey hesitated just a second. "Just some practice. The bartender," she added with a tilt of her chin. "She's got great bone structure."

Michel leaned in slightly. "Yes. There's something Grecian in her features. Like a forgotten oracle."

Pati, overhearing from a few feet away, nearly rolled her eyes.

Casey let out an awkward laugh. "That's… poetic."

"I've always been drawn to expressions," he said. "The way the face holds something long after the eyes stop seeing."

Phillip turned just enough to angle his shoulder between Michel and Casey. Not aggressively. Just enough to say: That's close enough.

"Hey man, she's already got her Frenchman," Phillip said, with a tone that seemed to be half joking, half serious.

Pati poured a beer for a guy at the far end and moved back toward their side of the bar, towel in hand, pretending to tidy. Really, she just didn't want to miss anything. She could feel it in her gut again—that buzz. Not from Tom's half-baked murder tale, not from the leftover humidity outside. This was something else. Michel looked… placed. As if someone had drawn him into the scene with deliberate pencil lines.

"You down here for Fantasy Fest?" Pati asked, leaning over to grab a bottle opener. "Or is this just a tropical sabbatical?"

Michel sipped his wine before answering. "I suppose you could call it that. I'm… recovering."

"From what?" she asked. Too direct, maybe, but the question slipped out.

He smiled without showing his teeth. "Work. City noise. Myself."

"Well," Pati said, setting down the towel, "we've got plenty of distractions for all three."

"And what would the best distraction be?"

Before Pati could respond, though she did have an at-ready list for the tourists that asked this question, Big Tom, who had been eavesdropping while pretending to scroll his phone, chimed in from down the bar.

"The Red Garter Saloon," Big Tom snorted.

"Oh, c'mon, Tom," the drunkard next to him said, slapping Big Tom's big back. "He looks a bit fancy for Paulina and Sandra, don't you think?"

"I think any man can appreciate tits like theirs," Big Tom snorted again. He always seemed to laugh at himself, even when he wasn't fully, and that laugh sounded more like a pig grunt.

Michel plastered a tight smile on his face. It was forced, almost condescending. "Perhaps something a bit more cultural?"

Pati, finally able to interject, said, "There's Hemingway House."

"Oh," Michel said, with piqued interest. "You know he's big up in Toronto, too."

"I did not know that," Pati admitted. "But it's a pretty neat Historic Landmark, and there's like a million six-toed cats around."

"I have a nasty cat allergy, so I suppose that won't do

either," Michel said flatly.

"The lighthouse museum is interesting," Casey added. "After Phillip and I got together, we went on a date there. I really enjoyed it."

"Ooh! Now that's more like it," Michel's body seemed to vibrate in his barstool, his body becoming more erect as if an electric shock had just gone through it. "I do love old nautical tales."

"You want a nautical tale?" Big Tom snorted back into the conversation. "How about the body they found up in Islamorada?"

Michel turned to him with perfect calm. "Yes, I heard. Tragic."

Tom leaned forward. "They say it looked almost… posed. You ever hear of anything like that up your way?"

"I've heard of worse," Michel said, his voice flat. "I once saw the aftermath of a cult killing—the leader said the moon made him do it."

That shut Tom up for a full three seconds—an accomplishment.

Phillip raised an eyebrow. "You sound like someone who's seen a lot."

Michel's gaze drifted toward the window, where a lizard clung upside-down to the screen. "I've seen enough to know when to stay quiet."

Pati's unease bloomed into something more pointed. She didn't think he was dangerous. But she couldn't shake the sense that he was rehearsed. As if every word came from a script he'd studied long before he stepped off the plane.

She went to stack a tray of pint glasses but kept one eye on the new stranger in her bar. Michel stood, almost reverently, leaving his class on the bar. He made his way toward the jukebox in the corner—a hulking Rowe CD classic, its lights dimmed by age but still glowing like a shrine. Regulars knew it as the heart of the Parrot, a time machine loaded with everything from New Orleans funk to rare reggae cuts and forgotten alt-country gems. Most tourists didn't touch it. Locals treated it like it was sacred. But Michel approached like a man on pilgrimage, pressing buttons with the precision of someone who'd memorized the map. He paused, waited for the old gears to whirl to life, then stepped back as the machine answered him.

A pause. A mechanical click.

And then, from the speaker in the corner, the soft crackle of a song cueing up—old, fuzzy, familiar.

"La Vie en Rose."

The grain of it stretched like smoke across the bar. Slow, slow notes. The kind of tune that made everything still for a second, the world holding its breath in French.

Michel didn't return to his seat right away. He stood there, hands folded in front of him, as if listening for something no one else could hear. Not the melody, but something buried underneath it. A memory. A voice.

Pati felt a ripple crawl up her spine. Not fear. Not yet. But something ancestral. Something that didn't like being this quiet in the middle of a busy bar.

Phillip looked up sharply, like a tuning fork had been struck near his head.

Casey reached for her sketchpad again, her pencil suddenly moving faster.

Pati, towel in hand, glanced toward the door and caught her own reflection in the glass—blurred by daylight, framed by dusty neon.

Somewhere out there, a girl had been left for the tide. Blue eyes open. Hands folded. Whispering to the moon. And now this man with the French accent, the pressed shirt, and the still hands had walked into her bar in the off-season. Something just didn't feel right.

The song had ended ten minutes ago, but Pati could still feel it in the walls.

Michel had finished his drink, thanked her politely and left before dark, walking off in that unhurried, deliberate way that made her itch. She wasn't sure if he'd paid in cash or card—she'd check the till later.

The bar had filled up a little more since sunset. A couple of tattooed Coasties had taken over the end of the bar. An exhausted bachelorette group was trying to revive themselves with coconut water and fries. And Big Tom had, mercifully, relocated to a quieter stool, where someone was humoring him with a story about a Fantasy Fest costume that involved a live iguana and a snorkel mask.

The shift change came like a breeze through a hot room. It was five o'clock somewhere and that somewhere was here and now. Pati's relief, Rachel, arrived ten minutes early, hair damp from a quick rinse and smelling like coconut shampoo and cigarette smoke.

"You look like someone who got ghosted by a bottle of red," Rachel said, slinging her purse behind the bar. That was how Rachel and Pati described the feeling of utter dismay and confusion. It was Rachel who had originally been "ghosted by a bottle of red" but then it was a literal bottle of red her drunk ass was drinking straight out of after getting ghosted by yet another online frat boy who was only in town for the week anyway. She definitely set it down somewhere and walked away, but Rachel leaned into the drama and poetry of life. So ghosted by a bottle of red it was.

Pati handed off the towel. "You ever get a vibe off someone that just... doesn't land right?"

Rachel snorted. "This whole island's one big weird vibe. You'll have to narrow it down."

Pati gave her the quick rundown—French Canadian, pressed shirt, jukebox resurrection, "La Vie en Rose."

Rachel shrugged. "Sounds romantic."

"Sounds rehearsed," Pati muttered, grabbing her bag from the hook under the bar. "You're up. I need to get some air before I start imagining more bodies in the mangroves."

Rachel saluted, already halfway to the tap.

Pati didn't say goodbye to the regulars. They'd see her again tomorrow. She stepped out the side door, into the warmth of the evening.

The air smelled of salt and car exhaust and whatever floral incense a nearby crystal shop next door had been burning all day. The sidewalks glistened faintly with the memory of afternoon rain. A few roosters strutted under the dim orange glow of streetlamps like they owned the island—which, in a way, they did.

She unlocked her bike from the rack by the alley. It was an old cruiser with one squeaky pedal and faded bumper stickers up the frame. It fit her. She started pedaling toward the bridge to her home, the island adjacent to Key West—Stock Island—and the light of the bars and noise of the crowds began to dim behind her, the warm dark ahead.

It was the part of the night she liked best. Just her and the road, the soft whir of tires, and the occasional whisper of the tide on her left. The breeze was sticky but moving. Somewhere, wind chimes jangled in a backyard garden. The moon was still low, but climbing. She hadn't realized how tightly her shoulders had been drawn until they started to loosen.

She passed the RV park, then the sign for Cow Key Channel, the path narrowing just enough to remind her how close the water was on either side. Most nights, it felt freeing.

Tonight, it felt like crossing a line she wouldn't be able to uncross. She was halfway across the bridge when her phone buzzed in the pocket of her canvas bag.

She coasted to a stop, pulled it out, and frowned. The number on the screen wasn't saved—just ten digits she didn't recognize, glowing up at her in the dark. For a second, she considered letting it ring out. The breeze from the channel was warm against her skin, and she didn't want whatever it was—telemarketer, wrong number, ghost of bad decisions—getting in the way of her peace. But something—intuition maybe, or just habit—made her swipe to answer.

"Hello?"

"Pati?"

She froze.

"Yeah… Who's this?"

"It's Danny."

She didn't say anything for a beat. The voice was the same—calm, measured, a little too practiced. But the number had thrown her.

"New phone?" she asked, trying to keep it light.

"New number," he said. "Clara kicked me off the plan."

That landed with a strange weight.

"She, uh… she said if we were going to take space, it should be real. Couldn't even keep my number—go figure."

Pati shifted her weight, foot balancing on the edge of the bike pedal. Below her, the tide sloshed softly against the pylons. A car passed on the opposite side of the bridge, its headlights flaring then fading.

"So… things are that bad?"

He exhaled. "Yeah. They're not great. I'm not calling to dump it all on you, I swear. I just—I need to get out of Nashville for a while. Thought maybe I could come down, clear my head, sleep on your couch a couple nights. If that's okay."

The wind picked up slightly, rustling the hem of her shirt and the palm fronds in the distance. She looked out across the dark water toward the faint scatter of lights on Stock Island. She hadn't seen Danny in years. Not since Danny's birthday trip, where he convinced Clara to rent that weird Airbnb in Big Pine Key with the haunted bathroom mirror and she and Clara had gotten into a screaming match about rum cake.

Pati didn't answer right away.

"Just a couple nights," he added. "If it's weird, I'll get a motel. I just… I didn't know where else to go."

She looked back the way she'd come, toward the bars and the buzz and the jukebox still echoing faintly in her bones. And then forward, toward the dim quiet of her borrowed rental and the couch she sometimes fell asleep on watching late-night crime documentaries.

"Yeah," she said. "Okay. You can stay a couple nights. Don't make me regret it."

"Never," he said quickly. "Thanks, Pati. Really. I'll text when I get in."

She hung up, slid the phone back into her canvas

bag, and sat there for another minute, balanced between islands, between tides. Then she pushed off and started pedaling again—back into the dark, where the air was quieter but her thoughts weren't.

CHAPTER 2
THE MAN FROM UP NORTH

The Green Parrot always felt like a different bar in the morning. With the lights off and the sound down, it was just a big old room with a sticky floor, a few ghosts clinging to the walls, and the faintest smell of last night's rum.

Pati unlocked the front door and shoved her shoulder into it, hip-checking the swollen frame like always. It gave way with a familiar groan. She flipped on one row of lights and let the gray light from the overcast morning do the rest.

The heat was already sitting heavy on the air, the kind that made her tank top feel like a second skin by the time she crossed the room. Outside, the end of hurricane season was dragging its feet—storms building and collapsing before they made landfall, leaving everything just damp enough to feel mildewed. She liked the weirdness of October. The way the town turned theatrical, glittered in fake cobwebs, while real ones lingered in alleyways and rafters.

She lit the cinnamon incense behind the bar—not because she believed in the woo of it, but because it cut the sour mix smell from the night before—and started her opening routine. Glasses stacked, mats shaken out, fruit caddy restocked. She found a slice of lime hardened into something fossilized in the ice bin and flicked it into the trash like it had offended her.

As she brewed a fresh pot of coffee, she noticed the folded note beside the register. Rachel's chicken-scratch handwriting sprawled across the front: *Your French friend came back.*

Pati wiped her hands and unfolded it. *He came in around 9. Had two glasses of red. Quiet. No weirdness, just polite. Left a $10 tip on a $14 tab. Didn't talk to anyone. Gave me the creeps anyway. - Rach.*

Pati read it twice. Then she tucked the note under the register and stared out the window at the wet sidewalk, trying to name what she felt.

It wasn't fear. Not exactly.

It was the same feeling she got when the tide came in too fast, or when a storm changed direction mid-track. That low hum of something's coming, even when the sky still looked calm.

She shook it off and focused on the rest of the prep. When she turned on the music, she skipped past any-thing French. Settled on a mellow island playlist—steel drums and lo-fi reggae.

She told herself she wasn't thinking about Michel. Not really. He was just another weirdo passing through. The bar saw hundreds of them every year. The problem with guys like that was they stuck to your ribs. Polite, composed, good posture—like he'd been assembled for a dinner party and sent to the wrong event.

And the song. God, the song.

Even thinking about the way "La Vie en Rose" had crackled out of the jukebox made her stomach pull tight. Not because of the melody—plenty of songs hit like ghosts—but because of the timing. The hush in the room. The way he'd looked when he played it, not moved, just listened. Like he was waiting for someone to answer it back.

By the time the first regular walked in—a bearded carpenter named Julian who always ordered a black coffee and a shot of Jameson—she had shoved the thoughts aside and settled into her usual groove. She even smiled.

"You're up early," she said, pouring him his usual.

"Didn't sleep," Julian grunted, dropping into a barstool like it had insulted him.

"Storm keep you up?"

"Something did."

She didn't press. If there was one thing she'd learned working bars, it was that most people would either spill everything or nothing—if you waited long enough. The bar began to wake up around her, slowly but surely. Another regular or two trickled in. The front door creaked with the weight of the humidity, and someone outside was already blasting Jimmy Buffett from a golf cart.

Just another morning in Key West.

Soon Mimi was busting through the door for her mid-morning Bloody Mary and crossword puzzle time at the bar. Pati liked Mimi. She had three Bloody Marys, all made spicy. You replaced her drink twice and didn't say a damn word to her. She tipped well, unless you asked her what she needed. God forbid you do ask, as a newbie bartender did during training once.

"I need my second Bloody Mary and for you to get the fuck out of my face." Mimi almost felt like she belonged in a pub in New York City, but here she was living her best life in Key West.

Pati instinctively began making a Bloody Mary after seeing Mimi, and by the time the old woman got to her seat at the bar—beacuse she did have her seat—Pati was placing it in front of her. Mimi pulled out her crosswords and got to work.

Pati ran her towel along the bartop, watching the door but pretending like she wasn't. After reading Rachel's note, she was worried Michel would make the Parrot his regular hangout while he was in town. Pati was preparing herself, so when the door opened again, bringing with it a gust of warm air and the scent of yesterday's storm rising off the street, she didn't even flinch when Michel walked in.

Michel stepped inside like he belonged to a slower decade—calm, upright, no sunglasses despite the glare bouncing off the wet pavement outside. His shirt was another button-down, this time pale blue, sleeves rolled precisely to his elbows. He wore slacks again, which felt like a crime in this humidity.

He nodded to Pati as he approached the bar. "Good morning."

She gave him a neutral look, towel still in hand. "Barely."

"True," he said, settling on a stool. "But the day feels longer here. More light, more time."

Pati r esisted the urge to reply, *You sound like a fortune cookie.* Instead, she reached for the coffee pot. "Want a cup?"

He looked at it like she'd offered him engine oil. "Actually… if you don't mind—red wine again."

"Before noon?" Pati served all kinds of things before noon, but wine usually wasn't on the list.

"I've always found coffee a bit aggressive. Wine has patience."

"Do you say shit like that on purpose?"

Michel smiled gently. "Only when it's true."

She poured the wine. He accepted it with both hands, like it was sacred. Sipped. Closed his eyes.

Pati busied herself behind the bar, but her eyes kept flicking back to him. He wasn't doing anything wrong. Wasn't doing anything at all. Just sipping wine and writing in a little notebook with a fountain pen, of all things. It made her itch.

He glanced up once, catching her mid-stare. "Is there something on my face?"

Pati didn't flinch, just shifted her weight and kept drying the same glass she'd been working over for the past minute.

"Nah," she said. "Just figuring you for a coffee guy. Or maybe tea, something herbal."

He tilted his head slightly, amused. "Why's that?"

"Wine before noon's not exactly rare around here," she said. "But it's usually coming from someone who smells like old socks and mutters about lizard people. You don't strike me as the type."

Michel chuckled—soft, contained, almost rehearsed. "That's reassuring."

"It's not a compliment," she added. "Just means I can't place you yet."

He didn't respond right away. Just took another slow sip from the glass, like he had all the time in the world.

Outside, the rain had held off for the morning, but the clouds still loomed—thick and low like they hadn't made up their minds. The kind of weather that made tourists antsy and locals wary.

"I like how the morning tastes here," he said after a pause. "Even when it's hot. The air carries stories. The walls, too."

Pati raised a brow. "You writing a travel blog or just trying out lines?"

Michel smiled without showing teeth. "Neither. Just an observation."

She didn't say anything. Didn't need to. She'd worked

this bar long enough to know when someone was full of shit, and when someone was simply hard to read. Michel wasn't the kind of weird that set off alarms. He was the kind that made you keep your knife sharp just in case.

Still. He wasn't drinking fast. He wasn't leering or lingering in that way some solo travelers did. He was just... unsettlingly composed.

She dropped the glass into the rack with a gentle clink and reached for the next.

"You always this cryptic, or is that just a vacation thing?"

Michel looked around the mostly empty bar, as if considering the weight of the room.

"Sometimes quiet places ask for quieter answers," he said.

And before she could roll her eyes or reply with something biting, the door creaked open and let in a rush of sunlight, damp air, and the faint jingle of a bicycle bell.

The front door opened again, and there he was.

Sweaty, sun-flushed, and grinning like a kid who just found a shortcut through the woods: Danny.

He pushed the door all the way open with his shoulder, holding the handlebars of a beat-up cruiser bike with peeling teal paint and one crooked handle grip. He wore cargo shorts, a damp T-shirt, and a look that made it very clear he wasn't sorry for the entrance.

"Found you," he said, breathless but cheerful.

Pati blinked. "Danny?"

"Surprise," he said, parking the bike just inside the doorway like this was normal.

She set the bar towel down slowly, staring at him like he might dissolve if she moved too fast.

"You're already here?" she asked. "What the hell?"

"I took the first flight out this morning," he said, running a hand through his damp hair. "Just grabbed my backpack and left."

She glanced around as if the backpack might be somewhere in the bar.

"I went by your place first," he added, "but you weren't there. So I rode here."

"You biked from the airport to Stock Island…" she said slowly, pointing at him, "and then, when I wasn't home… you biked all the way back here?"

Danny grinned. "Well—I left my backpack over your fence, so I didn't have to bring that. But yeah!"

Pati just stared at him for another beat, then shook her head and walked around the bar. She didn't hug him— yet—but she took the bike from his hands and wheeled it back outside, propping it near the railing. *Where did he even get this thing?* she wondered.

When she came back in, he was already perched on a stool, waving politely to Mimi and Julian like they were old friends, and nodding at Michel like he wasn't still visibly sweating from a ten-mile ride across the damn island chain.

She dropped a glass of ice water in front of him.

"You're a lunatic," she said.

Danny shrugged. "Felt like a good idea."

Michel, who had watched the exchange with a polite sort of curiosity, lifted his glass slightly. "Quite the entrance."

Danny smiled at him. "Well, I don't usually get introductions like a bicycle bell in a bar, but I figure if you can't roll with it in Key West, you're doing it wrong."

Michel tilted his head. "Are you also visiting?"

"Something like that," Danny said, then turned to Pati. "You said I could crash a few nights, right?"

"I did," she muttered, more to herself than anyone else. Then, louder: "You still only eat peanut butter and toast, or did you evolve?"

Danny leaned back on the barstool, looking out the window like he'd just arrived at a vacation he didn't plan. "I'm easy. But if you've got coffee, I won't fight you on it."

Pati poured him a cup without another word. But her mind was spinning. She hadn't expected him until at least the next day, maybe later. She definitely hadn't expected this—all charm and chaos, unshowered and smiling, like none of it was complicated.

But it was complicated.

She handed him the coffee. "You're dripping sweat on my bar."

Danny grinned again. "Feels good to be here."

Pati didn't answer. She just leaned back against the cooler, eyes shifting between Danny and Michel. One too familiar. One not familiar enough. And the air between them held just the slightest weight—like the storm clouds still thinking about whether to break.

Pati lifted the heavy crate of glass bottles that were piling up beneath the bar, lugged them to the back, and nudged the swinging door with her hip. The bottles clinked with every step as she made her way toward the side alley where the recycling bins sat beneath a half-dead banana tree and a mural of a rooster in sunglasses.

She didn't expect him to follow her. But she should have.

The screen door creaked open a second later, and Danny stepped out, still sipping the last of his water like it was a cocktail.

"You still take this stuff out yourself?" he asked.

Pati didn't look at him. "I like the excuse to get away from people for five minutes."

Danny leaned against the frame of the door for a beat before pushing it closed and joining her by the bins.

"Let me," he said, reaching for the crate.

She pulled it just out of reach. "I've got it."

He didn't argue. Just stood there while she dumped the bottles into the blue bin one by one, letting the sharp sound of glass hitting glass fill the space between them.

When she finished, she set the crate down on the lid with a thunk and wiped her hands on the towel tucked into her back pocket.

"I didn't think you'd actually come this fast," she said.

"I didn't think I would either," Danny replied. "But then I bought a ticket at two in the morning and didn't stop to second-guess it."

Pati crossed her arms. "You said you needed a couch, not an intervention."

"I know." He paused. "But you said yes."

She looked at him, arms still crossed. "I said yes because I've always liked you."

Danny opened his mouth, then shut it.

"But you know this is weird, right?" she added. "I mean… you're Clara's husband. Or whatever you are now. And she's my sister."

"I know it's weird."

"We don't even talk," Pati said quickly, like she had to get ahead of her own guilt. "Clara and me. We haven't really talked in, like, years. Our texts are just holidays and the occasional one-word reaction to a wedding photo someone else posted."

Danny nodded slowly. "Yeah. I know how she is."

Pati turned to him, her eyes sharp now. "That's not what I meant."

He looked away, toward the fence where a few lizards sunned themselves on a post.

"I just meant," she continued, "that she's still my sister. Even if she's cold and judgmental and thinks bartending is a cry for help."

Danny cracked a smile at that. "She did say that once."

"Yeah. At her own engagement dinner."

They were both quiet for a second. A car drove by on Whitehead Street, tires splashing through a left-over puddle.

"I'm not here to put you in the middle," Danny said, finally. "I'm not trying to drag you into anything. I just… I don't know. I missed you."

Pati sighed, leaned her shoulder against the wall. "You missed Key West."

"I missed both."

That hung there for a moment. Neither of them moved.

"You're not sleeping on the couch forever," she said.

"I wouldn't dream of it."

"You clean up your sweat puddle on the bar before you die of heatstroke?"

"Mostly," Danny said with a sheepish grin. "That ride was a little longer than I thought."

"You think?" She looked at him again. "Where'd you even get that piece-of-shit thing?"

"Eh, a kid was selling it."

"You really bought a bike from a kid on the side of the road?"

"Two kids," he said. "Fifteen bucks. No brakes."

"Jesus Christ."

"But the bell works."

She shook her head. "You're lucky you're still charming."

"I try."

They both smiled, but only for a moment.

Then she pushed off the wall and reached for the empty crate.

"Come on," she said. "You can earn your keep by refilling the ice bins. And not making it weird when Clara finds out you're here."

Danny followed her back toward the bar, quiet again. But something in her gut tugged, just slightly. Something that told her weird was already in motion.

CHAPTER 3
SOMEWHERE ON THE CHAIN

The sign at Captain Tony's glowed soft and gold beneath a string of flickering Halloween lights, half of them already tangled in plastic cobwebs and sun-faded from last October. A three-piece band strummed through a sleepy cover of Come Monday, and the usual mix of locals, boat bums, and in-the-know tourists lingered around the bar.

Cool as a crypt, dark as a cellar, and stitched together with decades of haze, music, and muttered secrets. The stone floor held onto chill like memory, and the low ceilings turned every voice into a whisper if you didn't push it through with purpose.

Pati leaned her elbows on the bar, the wood worn smooth under her forearms, her second drink sweating beside her. Danny sat beside her, freshly showered and finally looking like he'd stopped moving. He had on a faded gray T-shirt and cargo shorts, his sandals damp from the sidewalk. His posture said "vacation." His eyes said something else, but she didn't feel like looking too hard tonight.

From behind the bar, Sam smirked as he slid over a whiskey, neat. His dark hair was buzzed short, his sleeves rolled up, a bar towel slung over one shoulder like a battle flag.

"You look like a woman who just wrestled an iguana out of a cooler," Sam said, popping open a soda water for himself.

"Close," Pati said, accepting the drink. "It was a bachelorette party from Jacksonville, which is basically the same thing."

Sam leaned his elbows on the bar. "Fantasy Fest hasn't even started and already the freaks are blooming."

Pati gestured vaguely toward Danny. "Case in point."

Danny raised his glass. "I take that as a compliment."

Sam gave him a glance, his expression somewhere between suspicion and mild approval. "Don't think we've met."

"Danny," he said. "Houseguest. Longtime mistake. Couch surfer deluxe."

"He's Clara's ex or husband; I'm honestly not sure," Pati added flatly.

Sam's eyebrows lifted. "That Danny? Birthday trip Danny?"

"Yep," Pati said.

"Damn," Sam said, then gave her a look. "And you let him back into your life why, exactly?"

Danny laughed. "I've got good manners and decent taste in beer."

Pati rolled her eyes and drained half her glass.

Danny pushed off his stool. "I'm gonna step outside, see if the weed cart guy's still around. Back in a few."

He ducked out with a wave, letting a spill of streetlight in behind him before the heavy door thudded closed again, dropping them back into the cool hush.

Sam gave Pati a look.

"What?"

"Just making sure you know what the hell you're doing."

"I don't," Pati said. "But I'm too tired to regret it yet."

Sam smirked and topped off her glass. "Cheers to consistency."

They clinked glasses. Pati let herself sink into the silence for a minute. The bar was cool, the light low, and for the first time all day, her spine had stopped coiling.

Then the guy next to her said, almost casually, "Did you hear about the body they found in Marathon?"

She didn't turn to look at him. Not yet.

Just stared into her glass and felt her stomach drop, one slow degree at a time.

The guy who'd spoken was nursing a rum and coke, arms tanned, probably mid-50s, wearing a faded dive shop T-shirt and a conch shell necklace. He had the leathery skin of someone who'd never heard of SPF and the low, gravelly voice of a bar regular who'd seen enough weird things in the Keys not to get spooked easily.

"What do you mean, a body?" Sam asked. "I mean, another one?"

"Marathon," the guy said. "Word is she was found just

north of Seven Mile Bridge this morning. Real pretty. Young. Same as the one from Islamorada."

Someone else—a tourist in a Parrothead tee—cut in from a nearby barstool. "I heard about the Islamorada one. She was… posed, right?"

The first guy nodded. "Hair fanned out in the sand, hands folded like she was waiting on a damn wedding photographer. This one too, from what I heard. And their hands were bound with rope. I think I heard both were strangled too."

Someone farther down muttered, "Two girls in a week? Same county?"

"Same setup?" the Parrothead added.

Pati crossed her arms. "So either it's the same guy moving south, or it's someone who wants it to look that way."

"Or," Sam said, glancing over, "it's someone who never left. Could've been down here the whole time. Islamorada and Marathon aren't far drives from here."

That quieted them for a moment.

Captain Tony's suddenly felt colder than usual. The low ceiling, comforting just minutes before, seemed to press in like a lid.

"Heard the cops found somethin' even weirder with this one," he said. "She had somethin' in her hand. A bit of driftwood, maybe? With writing on it."

Pati blinked. "What kind of writing?"

"Some lyric or quote. Something about the moon."

Her stomach flipped. Hadn't that weird Michel guy

said something about a moon cult killing? What if he was really responsible?

Sam caught it—her shift in posture, her stillness. "You all right?"

She nodded, but barely. "Just… tired."

"Sure," Sam said, but he didn't look away.

Just then, Danny reappeared—swinging through the door with a gust of stale heat, looking far too chipper for someone walking into a murder conversation.

He dusted his hands. "Well, that guy out front's got the good stuff. Got a pre-roll if anyone's interested."

A few heads turned, distracted, maybe grateful.

Danny flopped back into his stool, picked up his half-drunk beer, and looked around. "What'd I miss?"

Pati didn't answer. Neither did Sam.

The old man at the bar said, "You might wanna start locking your doors at night, friend."

Danny raised an eyebrow. Sam just shook his head and returned to wiping down the bar.

"Keys folks don't like to admit how many drifters blend in. You put on flip-flops and a fake tan, nobody questions a damn thing."

It was nearing eleven by the time they made it back to Pati's. The heat of the day had finally relented, but the air still hung heavy with the kind of warm stickiness that clung to your skin. The sounds of the island were quieter at night: distant dogs barking, the low hum of insects, and the occasional sputter of a scooter wheezing past on the main drag

Danny collapsed onto the weather-worn couch on Pati's screened-in porch, cracked open a beer from her fridge, and tilted his head back with a satisfied sigh. "Now this," he said, "this is more like it."

Pati, barefoot and in an oversized tank top, perched on the armchair across from him, her own bottle sweating in her hand. She looked tired but wired, the kind of buzz that didn't come from alcohol.

"You remember that guy this morning? The one at the Parrot with the accent?" she asked.

Danny squinted. "The one drinking red wine?"

"Yeah. Michel. From Quebec."

"Right. The Hemingway wannabe."

Pati let out a sharp laugh. "I can't decide if he's just some weirdo on vacation or…I don't know. He's…off."

Danny lifted an eyebrow.

"No, really," Pati said. "Hear me out. Okay. The other night he was in on my shift, I left around five, and he left before me. But then he came back in a few hours later; Rachel left me a note."

"And tourists don't revisit bars they enjoyed?"

"Ugh. I don't know," Pati relented. "But it was something about him. It was more than that. There was something in the way he moved. Still. Like a guy pretending to be human."

Danny chuckled, but there was unease behind his grin. "You sure you're not just creeped out from all the murder talk tonight?"

"I've been bartending in the Keys for a decade," she said flatly. "I've seen drunk, I've seen weird, I've seen people having full-on hallucinations in my bar and thought nothing of it. But this guy... he gave me goosebumps."

Danny took another pull of his beer. "What exactly did he do?"

"He came in, ordered red wine, inserted himself into a conversation two of my regulars were having, and, oh my god, that was creepy too," Pati said, remembering something else Michel had said.

"What? What is it?" Danny asked.

"One of those regulars—Casey—she's an artist. Well, so is her boyfriend Phillip. Well, it doesn't matter. Casey was sketching at the bar, and that dude, Michel, went over, asked to see her sketch, which was evidently a sketch of my hand. And that weirdo started on about me having Grecian features; he mentioned an oracle or something. It was so creepy."

"Okay, I'll give you that one. That's weird as hell," Danny said.

"It gets worse," Pati continued. "He used the jukebox to put on this dusty old version of 'La Vie en Rose,' and stood there, like... like it was some kind of altar."

Danny paused mid-sip. "Wait—'La Vie en Rose'?"

"Yeah. You know it?"

He let out a bark of laughter. "That was our wedding song. Me and Clara."

Pati blinked, thrown. "Seriously?"

"Yeah," Danny said, shaking his head. "Clara picked it. Said it was romantic, timeless. I barely knew what it meant. I think I spilled my drink on her dress during the first chorus."

Pati sat back, stunned. "I forgot that was your song."

"You probably didn't care."

"Not really," she admitted. "Clara wanted the wedding to be perfect. Everything white and blush pink and symmetrical. I showed up on time, wore the ugly dress she picked, and slipped out before cake."

Danny smiled. "You always hated that kind of stuff."

"She always hated that I hated it."

They sat in silence for a beat, the cicadas buzzing in rhythm with the clink of glass bottles against lips.

"So what, you think this Michel guy had the same wedding song as you and Clara?" Pati asked, voice low.

"It's not exactly a deep cut for anyone with an affinity for French culture like your sister," Danny said. "But it's weird. I'll give you that."

Pati rubbed at her temple. "I know I sound paranoid. But that song playing... the way he stood there in reverence. The way he looked like he was somewhere else entirely."

"Maybe he was," Danny said. "Maybe it reminds him of someone."

"Maybe it does," she echoed.

Another long pause stretched between them.

"Anyway," Danny added, finishing his beer, "he doesn't seem like a killer. Just a pretentious tourist with a tragic backstory."

Pati didn't respond. She stood, stretching her arms above her head.

"I'm beat," she said. "You can crash out here if you want. There's a pillow and a blanket in the wicker trunk. Or feel free to go inside if it gets too muggy. There's blankets and pillows on the couch."

Danny saluted her with his bottle. "Much obliged."

She hesitated at the door, looking back at him. "I mean it, Danny. Be careful. Something feels off. And it's not just Michel."

Danny nodded, more sober now. "I will. Promise."

Pati disappeared inside, screen door clicking shut behind her.

Danny leaned back against the couch, gazing out through the screen at the flickering porch light and the night beyond. Then he looked down at his bottle, swirled the last mouthful of beer, and muttered, "'La Vie en Rose,' huh?"

He set the bottle down, and the porch settled into stillness. Outside, the warm wind carried the faintest sound of waves against the shore. And in the dark, he started humming.

CHAPTER 4
SHORELINE WHISPERS

The room was hot when Pati woke, the kind of heat that told her she'd slept through the best part of the day and it was already the afternoon. Her sheets were tangled around one ankle, her mouth dry with the lingering taste of whiskey and unease. For a moment she didn't move, just let the ceiling fan slice the air above her in lazy circles.

Then her phone buzzed.

She reached for it with the sluggish reflexes of someone not quite ready to be awake. The screen glowed too bright. One new message, from Rachel.

Another one. Stock Island. You okay?

Pati sat up straight. The haze lifted in an instant. Her heart kicked up and sweat beaded under her arms.

Stock Island.

She pushed off the sheets and padded barefoot across the room, pulling up shorts as she hobbled across the floor. The tile floor was warm, sun-soaked. She cracked open her bedroom window. Outside, everything looked normal—bright bougainvillea, a neighbor's rooster strutting along the fence line, the distant bark of a dog.

But nothing felt normal.

She walked through the living area and opened the back door to the patio room. Danny's pillow was still crumpled on the couch, the blanket half-kicked off. But no Danny.

Pati stepped outside, shading her eyes. "Danny?"

No answer.

She checked the bathroom. Nothing. Walked a slow circle around the house, calling his name. That little twist of fear started building again, like it had when she saw Rachel's message.

Then she caught movement out of the corner of her eye—past the tangle of palm and banana leaves in the backyard, beyond the old fishing crate she used as a planter.

Danny, fast asleep in the hammock, limbs sprawled in every direction like he'd been thrown there by a storm. One arm dangled low, a bottle of water still clutched in his hand.

Pati exhaled hard through her nose and leaned against the porch rail.

"Jesus Christ," she muttered.

He snorted awake at the sound, eyes fluttering open. "Is it Tuesday?"

"It's Thursday."

"Oh." He squinted. "That feels wrong."

She didn't answer. Just turned back inside and poured a mug of coffee from the half-full pot she'd forgotten to empty the night before.

Rachel's message sat there on the screen, taunting her.

Pati typed back: *Yeah. I'm okay. Trying to wrap my head around it.*

Then she stared out the window, toward the thin stretch of mangroves and boatyards that separated her little house from the shoreline.

Another one. And this time, on her home island.

By the time Pati made it to Hogfish Bar & Grill, the sun was baking the crushed shell lot out front and every wooden table inside buzzed with a mix of locals, service workers, and fishermen still shaking off their last charter. It was her day off, and she didn't want to sit at home listening to Danny snore the afternoon away.

Pati slid onto a barstool and gave her cropped hair a quick push back with one hand. She hadn't even brushed it this morning—just splashed cold water on her face, pulled on a soft tank and cutoff shorts, and left Danny mumbling in the hammock.

Lena, the first-shift bartender, spotted her and gave a tight-lipped nod. "You want the usual?"

"Make it extra spicy," Pati said, voice lower than usual.

Lena raised an eyebrow but didn't ask. The Hogfish wasn't the Parrot. Here, people kept their questions to themselves and saved the real talk for after beer two.

The Bloody Mary came loaded: pickled green beans,

olives, shrimp, a wedge of lime. Pati stirred it absently, eyes drifting toward the TVs mounted above the bar.

Muted, but the headline on one caught her attention: THIRD BODY FOUND IN THE KEYS – YOUNG WOMAN DISCOVERED ON STOCK ISLAND.

The image behind it showed flashing lights near the shoreline, yellow tape fluttering in the early morning breeze. Pati looked away quickly. The rim of her glass was damp beneath her fingers.

"That's the third," someone said from a nearby table. A woman, maybe in her fifties, with a deep tan and a dive shirt. "They found her this morning, just down past the shrimp docks."

"Other side of the island from here," her companion added, a grizzled man with salt-and-pepper stubble. "But that's not saying much. Whole island's only what, two miles wide?"

Pati didn't mean to eavesdrop, but the conversation was happening just a few feet away—and now others were tuning in too. She recognized half the faces. Crew guys from the reef charters. A liveaboard couple from the marina. A pair of waitresses from Dantes still in last night's makeup.

"It's the same as the others?" someone asked. "Same setup?"

"Brown hair, blue eyes," said the woman. "Posed, just like the others. I heard from Tony—his cousin's wife is with the sheriff's office."

"You believe Tony?" someone snorted.

"He was right about that jet-ski bust last year."

"That was pure guesswork."

The conversation took off like dry kindling.

"I heard they've got a sketch."

"No way, they'd have posted that."

"They said the guy's under six foot, I swear."

"I heard someone saw her and a man walking along the shore around two a.m. Tall, dark clothes, maybe a hat."

"But it was dark."

"Yeah, and probably raining. Can't trust anything that early in the morning."

"I heard he's got an accent."

That snapped Pati back into focus.

She turned slightly in her seat. "What kind of accent?"

The dive shirt woman shrugged. "French, maybe? That's what Margo said. Her kid works graveyard at the Circle K. Said a guy came in real early this morning, all polite and quiet, asking for wine and batteries."

"Wine and batteries?" someone echoed.

"For what, a date and a homicide?"

"Could've just been camping," another voice offered.

Pati reached for her phone under the bar.

Her hands were clammy.

She texted Rachel: *Is Michel at the Parrot today?*

A beat.

Then: *Yeah. He's sitting at the bar right now. Why?*

Pati stared at the screen.

She could still hear the music. Someone had queued up "Tin Cup Chalice." It floated gently above the buzz of speculation.

"Jesus," someone at the end of the bar muttered. "What kind of guy kills three women and just… keeps hanging around?"

"The kind who wants to be caught."

"The kind who doesn't think he will be."

"Maybe he's not from here."

"Maybe he never left."

Pati sipped her drink, the vodka burning down slower than usual. The voices around her blurred together, until all she could hear was that one detail repeating: *He has a French accent.*

Pati parked her bike around the corner from the Green Parrot, heart thudding louder than she liked to admit. She could still hear the rumors ringing in her ears—*French accent, wine and batteries, brown hair, blue eyes.*

Pati paused on the sidewalk, wiping her palms on the hem of her tank top. It was too hot for nerves, but they clung to her anyway—sweaty, persistent, unwelcome. Pati took a breath, then another. Don't be weird. He's just a customer.

She stepped inside.

The bar smelled like limes, beer, and the faint tang of

old wood. Music trickled in from the back, just a warm-up riff, not yet showtime.

She spotted Rachel behind the bar and gave a tight nod. Rachel's eyebrows went up. She pointed with her chin—discreet, practiced.

Far end of the bar. Michel.

Pati didn't look right away. She made a show of checking the specials board, as if she didn't write them, then grabbed a stool halfway down. Rachel slid her a soda without asking, no questions, no commentary.

Then Rachel leaned in, whispering just loud enough for Pati to hear. "He's been nursing a glass of wine and scribbling in some little notebook. Keeps asking weird questions about the jukebox."

Pati blinked. "Like what kind of questions?"

"Like... does anyone ever change the selections, who decides what songs go on it, how often it's cleaned."

Pati frowned. "That's... specific."

Rachel nodded. "Creepy specific. You okay?"

"I will be," Pati said. "Just… keep him talking, if you can."

Rachel raised an eyebrow. "You want me to flirt with him?"

"No," Pati said quickly. "Just… I want to hear him. Watch him. See what he does."

"Got it," Rachel said, and moved off down the bar like it was any other shift.

Pati risked a glance.

There he was.

Michel sat alone, posture perfect, one hand wrapped delicately around a wine glass. His notebook was open in front of him—small, leather-bound, pages creased and stained like it had traveled a long way in a back pocket. He wore the same kind of shirt as yesterday: collared, pressed, just slightly too warm-looking for the weather.

He was speaking softly to Rachel now, gesturing toward the jukebox. She laughed politely, poured him a little more, then moved on.

Pati studied him. What's your deal?

She watched his eyes. Calm. Sharp. Every so often, they flicked toward the door. The jukebox. The hallway to the bathroom.

He didn't look nervous. He looked ready.

Michel reached into his pocket and pulled out a pair of earbuds. He tucked them in and stared ahead, completely still, mouth just barely moving.

Is he... singing?

Pati couldn't tell what he was listening to, but the faraway look in his eyes was the same one she'd seen the day before. The one that made her skin crawl.

She turned back to her soda and stared into the ice.

Her phone buzzed. A message from Danny: *U good? I can meet you.*

She typed back: *Stay home. I'm just watching someone.*

There was a long pause before he replied: *The Quebec guy?*

Pati didn't answer.

Because now Michel was packing up his notebook. Standing. Slipping his earbuds back into his shirt pocket. He dropped a tip—exactly four bills—and adjusted his sleeves before walking toward the exit.

She turned to Rachel. "How long was he here?"

Rachel shrugged. "Couple hours, on and off. Went outside for a smoke, came back in, same pattern."

"Did he talk to anyone?"

"Some tourist guy for a bit. They were trading song recommendations."

"Anything else weird?"

"Said it was one of the best jukeboxes he's ever seen. Talked about how rare it was to find a jukebox with that kind of range—and how surprised he was to find 'La Vie en Rose' on it."

Pati's brow creased. "That's the song he picked."

Rachel blinked. "Seriously? I thought he was just being poetic."

"He was more than poetic," Pati said quietly. "He looked like he was in a trance."

Rachel tilted her head. "Maybe it's sentimental?"

"Maybe," Pati murmured, thinking of Danny on the porch, beer in hand, laughing like it was nothing—*That was our wedding song.*

But this didn't feel like nostalgia. It felt like obsession. Like ritual.

Pati set her glass down and stood. "Let me know if he comes back tonight."

Rachel gave her a long look. "You okay?"

"No," Pati said honestly. "But I'm working on it."

She headed for the door, the cool hush of the bar replaced by the thick early evening air as she stepped outside.

Her phone buzzed again.

Danny: *You sure you don't want backup?*

Pati stared at the screen, thumb hovering.

Then she typed: *Nah. He's gone. Just keep an eye out.*

She slipped the phone into her pocket, rolled her shoulders back, and started walking. Behind her the jukebox clicked softly as a new song began.

She didn't see Michel on the sidewalk. Not immediately.

Pati's bike tires hummed softly over the uneven pavement, the faint click of her freewheel ticking in rhythm with the pulse at the base of her skull. She glanced left, then right—just people milling about in their evening sprawl, lingering tourists with sunburned shoulders and margaritas to-go, locals dragging out lawn chairs and six-packs, chasing what breeze they could before the night sealed shut with heat.

She would've ridden right past him if he didn't call out to her, bringing her to a complete halt.

"Oh! Pati! You're a bartender at the Green Parrot! Didn't I see you there tonight?"

"Oh, hi," Pati managed. "You're Michel, right? From

Quebec?" She was trying to play coy, as if she hadn't been semi-stalking him this afternoon.

"Yes, I am," he smiled, which made Pati uneasy. "And I did see you there tonight, didn't I? But you weren't working late last night or all day today—I've been stopping in for the occasional glass of wine, hoping to see you again. I find bartenders have the best stories about a town, and I'd love to hear yours."

"Yeah, uh, I had off today, and I typically work the earlier shift," Pati said, trying not to seem visibly creeped out.

"I imagine that's when many of your regulars come around," Michel said.

Pati nodded.

"Who knows! Maybe I'll move here and become a regular myself," he added.

Pati forced a smile. "You never know! But, hey, I've got to get going. Someone's waiting on me."

"Don't let me keep you," he smiled that too-calm smile again.

Pati began to pedal away. The sun was low, smearing orange over the rooftops and casting long shadows behind the palms. Even in October, the air was heavy. A stormy kind of thick, like the island was holding its breath. Pati pedaled harder.

She kept thinking about that jukebox. About how Michel had walked right to it. And when "La Vie en Rose" started to play, he didn't just listen. He drifted. Somewhere else. His eyes far off, his body almost too still. Like he was remembering something. Or worse—rehearsing it. And then all those questions about it today to Rachel? What was that about? He gave her the creeps, and now he had told her he was looking for her today. Great. She mentally scolded herself. *Why on earth did I tell him I worked the early shift most days? Damn the Catholic politeness that was beaten into me at such a young age.*

She turned onto the quieter road toward Stock Island. Traffic thinned fast. Out here, the air smelled more like salt and diesel. More like shrimp boats and oyster shells than sunscreen and spilled rum.

She welcomed it.

Still, her nerves hadn't quite settled. She reached the crest of the small bridge between the islands, standing on her pedals for the climb, and coasted on the other side. The water below caught the sun just right, flashing in gold streaks between the mangroves.

She was less than a mile from home when her phone buzzed in the basket. Pati stopped pedaling and let the bike coast as she reached for it. A message from Danny: *Where are you? I want to get lit tonight…Again.*

She frowned, typing back one-handed: *On my way. Just left Duval.*

A few seconds passed. Then: *Dinner? I picked up those weird empanadas you like.*

She smiled despite herself. Danny always remembered the little things. The coconut shrimp empanadas from that Cuban stand near the marina. Clara mocked them the last time they came down to visit. "Fried pocket grease," she called them. Which only made Pati like them more.

Be there in ten, she texted. She slipped the phone back into the basket and started pedaling again. The last stretch of the ride passed in silence. No more tourists, just the occasional dog barking from a fenced yard or a porch light clicking on. She turned down her street and pulled into the driveway, heart beating louder than she liked.

The house looked the same—nothing out of place, nothing strange. Just her modest yellow shotgun-style home with a drooping hibiscus bush near the front porch and the faint glow of a light inside. Danny must've flipped it on.

Pati swung off her bike, wheeled it up the path, and leaned it against the side of the house. As she reached the front door, she hesitated.

Was she being paranoid? Or had the island always felt this quiet after dark?

She stepped inside. Danny was in the kitchen, barefoot, a beer in one hand and a paper bag in the other. The empanadas were already on a plate, still steaming.

"Perfect timing," he said. "I was just about to start without you."

"You would've regretted it," Pati said, locking the door behind her. She kicked off her shoes and walked into the kitchen, her sweat-damp shirt clinging to her lower back.

Danny handed her a beer. "So?"

"So what?"

He studied her face. "How was the stakeout?"

Pati opened her mouth, then stopped.

She didn't know how to explain the way her skin crawled when Michel had looked her in the eyes. Instead, she took a bite of empanada. And chewed. And tried not to think about blue-eyed girls washing up on the shore.

CHAPTER 5
BONFIRES AND ALIBIS

Pati poured two whiskeys and handed one to Danny, who was sprawled across her porch couch like he had no intention of moving for the rest of the evening. The late sun bled orange across the sky, just visible through the screen.

"So," she said, settling into the armchair across from him, "you never told me what actually happened with Clara."

Danny took a long sip and then a longer pause. "What didn't happen?"

"Don't be evasive. I'm not her. I'm not gonna cry over your breakup or write about it in a Facebook post."

He chuckled. "You don't even have Facebook."

"Exactly."

He shifted, the old cushion wheezing beneath him. "We stopped seeing each other. Not like in the romantic sense—we literally stopped seeing each other. She'd be in bed before I got home, out the door before I woke up. We became... convenient strangers."

Pati raised her glass in a half-toast. "Romance isn't dead. It's just exhausted."

Danny laughed, but it caught in his throat. "She always hated the way I talked about feelings. Said I made everything into a joke so I didn't have to deal with it."

"Sounds like someone who desperately needed to relax."

"She never liked how relaxed I was," he said, tipping his head back. "Or how much I liked your laid-back little island world."

"That's probably why she married you," Pati said. "Thought she could turn you into someone uptight and shiny."

He smiled at her, soft and a little sad. "She tried."

Just then, Pati's phone buzzed on the porch railing. She leaned over and checked it.

Tia: *Bonfire party on Higgs tonight. You in?*

Pati grinned and held it up. "Tia from MoonDog. Bonfire at Higgs Beach. Want in?"

Danny shrugged. "Sure. I can bring my winning personality."

Pati typed back: *Can I bring Danny?*

Tia responded almost immediately: *Uh, duh?*

"Finish your drink," Pati said to Danny. "Then let's hit the road.

Danny finished his whiskey in one last gulp, and they headed out the door and onto their respective bicycles—Pati's in much better shape than the one Danny bought off those kids. As they rode, she mocked him for it.

"You know you could've rented a brand new bike,

dude," Pati laughed. "You didn't need to purchase that probably-stolen hunk of junk."

"Eh, I liked the charm of it," he said, ringing the bell that had announced his arrival just yesterday afternoon.

Man, it had been a long 36 hours, Pati thought.

They coasted past pastel houses and palm-lined streets, the warm air thick with the mingling smells of sea salt, distant grilling meat, and the occasional whiff of something herbal someone was definitely smoking on their porch. The sun had slipped behind the horizon, and now the sky glowed a deep bruise-purple overhead. A few early stars winked into view, blinking down like they weren't sure about committing yet.

Danny pedaled beside her, his posture loose and easy. "You know," he said, "I haven't felt this... unaccounted for in a long time."

Pati glanced over. "Is that a good thing?"

"I think so," he said. "It's like—I'm not trying to be anybody right now. Not the fixer. Not the guy who doesn't mind when Clara moves the furniture and tells me it's more feng shui. Not the one who's always fine. Just... me."

Pati scoffed. "You say that like it's profound, but I'm pretty sure you're just buzzed and pedaling toward a fire pit with a cooler full of beer."

"Hey, same difference," he said. "That's a spiritual journey where I'm from."

She grinned and gave her bike a little burst of speed to get ahead of him, laughing as he tried to catch up.

By the time they made it to Higgs Beach, the bonfire was already lit—its orange flames licking up toward the darkening sky, illuminating faces in warm flashes. Strings of café lights had been strung haphazardly between palm trees, and someone had dragged an old Bluetooth speaker onto the sand, playing something twangy and nostalgic. The party was already well underway—clumps of people standing around in flip-flops and cutoff shorts, passing drinks and stories like currency.

Tia spotted them from the drink table and waved them over.

"You made it!" she called. Then her smile faltered just a little. "Wait... who is this?"

Pati blinked. "My brother-in-law Danny. Clara's Danny."

Tia laughed awkwardly. "Oh my god. I thought you meant Danny the musician when you texted, but he's over there with his guitar and a cooler full of tequila. I was so confused."

Danny held up a hand. "No worries. I've been mistaken for other people before."

"Any chance you're going to do a cover of 'Margaritaville' like that Danny does?" Tia teased, pointing toward a beach bum with sun-bleached hair and a guitar on his lap.

"Depends on how many of these I drink." He grabbed a can off the table and popped the tab.

Tia gave him a look. "So... where's your wife?"

Danny took a long sip, then shrugged. "Probably somewhere perfectly decorated and emotionally distant."

Pati winced. "They're separated."

Tia's eyes widened. "Oh—shit. Sorry."

"It's fine," Danny said, waving it off. "That's why I'm here. Needed a little time away from... whatever the hell that was."

Tia nodded and smiled, slipping into hostess mode. "Well, come meet some folks. Plenty of weirdos to go around."

She led Danny off into the crowd, already launching into introductions.

Pati stayed back for a moment, letting the heat of the fire warm her shins. She watched Danny laugh at something Tia said, more alive than she'd seen him maybe ever. She wasn't sure if that made her feel better. Or worse.

By the bonfire, Tia led Danny into a loosely-formed semicircle of beach chairs and upside-down milk crates. "This is Ava and Rory," she said, nodding to a curly-haired woman in oversized glasses and a tall androgynous person.

"And that's the other Danny," she added, clapping the shoulder of a guy holding a battered acoustic guitar and tuning it like his life depended on it.

"Two Dannys?" Ava asked.

The musician looked up, grinning. "We're everywhere. It's a problem."

"Tell me about it," Pati's brother-in-law said. "It's why I came to the Keys. Danny overpopulation in the mainland."

Laughter rippled through the group. Musician Danny strummed a lazy chord. "Stick around, man. We'll teach you the secret handshake."

Danny raised his can in salute and took a sip. The drink tasted like sunscreen and mango vodka—par for the course.

Soon, he was absorbed in easy conversation. The kind that floated from sailing mishaps to bartending disasters to bad tattoos done after midnight. People here didn't ask where you were from unless it was to see if they knew someone you might've slept with. Nobody cared about résumés. Just stories.

Danny was mid-story about buying his bike off two middle schoolers when a new couple approached the fire.

"Yo, look who decided to show up!" someone shouted.

Casey and Phillip made their way over—Casey carrying a six pack of beers, Phillip trailing behind with the calm gravity of someone who always knew exactly where his center was. His arms were a canvas of black-and-grey ink, from a koi fish near his wrist to a dark cathedral spiraling up his shoulder. He wore a plain white tee that clung to his frame like it knew better than to wrinkle.

Danny didn't recognize them from the bar. Casey had a radiant, sun-freckled look of someone who'd been laughing more than crying lately. Phillip, meanwhile, looked like a Bond villain with better morals.

Casey handed off a beer and nodded to Danny. "You're Pati's in-law, right?"

"Technically," Danny said. "How'd you know that?"

"We just saw her on the walk in; she pointed you out," Casey winked.

Danny held out his hand. Casey shook it. "I'm Casey; this is Phillip."

Phillip nodded politely and murmured a soft greeting. His accent—French, faint, Mediterranean—slid into the air like a whisper.

Danny, trying to be funny, said, "Wait... French accent? Tall? Moody eyes? Aren't you a little on-the-nose for our mystery killer?"

Phillip raised one dark eyebrow, then smirked. "It's always the quiet ones."

Ava gasped dramatically. "Plot twist!"

Casey snorted. "Don't worry. I think I can vouch for where he's been the last few nights." She gave Phillip a mock-conspiratorial wink. "Unless he's been doing some moonlight murdering I don't know about."

"I don't multitask," Phillip said dryly. "Too stressful."

Everyone cracked up, and Danny relaxed into the ease of it all. Even the jokes about serial killers felt softer in the glow of a beach fire.

Soon, the guitar came back out. Someone handed around a harmonica and a tambourine, and a ragtag jam session formed like sea foam at the shore. Danny found himself sitting beside Tia again, the two of them watching the firelight ripple across the sand.

"So you liking it here?" she asked, brushing an invisible speck off her knee.

He shrugged. "It's weird. But good-weird."

Tia smiled. "That's kind of the tagline of this place."

He nodded toward the fire. "Everyone's been cool. Pati's been cool."

Tia gave him a side glance. "You two ever... y'know?"

Danny choked a little on his drink. "No. Never. Pati would murder me. And I think I'd deserve it."

"That's fair," Tia said, leaning back. "Just curious."

Danny smiled, a little flustered. "What about you? You seeing anyone?"

"I see a lot of people," she said with a smirk. "That doesn't mean I stop to talk to most of them."

"Smart."

A pause.

"But you stopped to talk to me."

"Don't let it go to your head."

They clinked bottles. The waves rolled in. And somewhere behind them, Pati was laughing with someone by the keg, already halfway to tomorrow.

Pati found Rachel over by the folding table someone had turned into an impromptu bar, where half-empty coolers sweated in the sand and a guy in a straw hat was performing a very serious canned margarita taste test. Rachel had her drink in one hand and was swatting at mosquitoes with the other.

"There you are," Pati said, holding up her beer in greeting.

"I didn't know you'd be out and about tonight; I figured you'd be entertaining your brother-in-law. Or is he still your brother-in-law? Ex brother-in-law?"

"Let's go with 'temporary house guest with emotional baggage.'"

Rachel laughed. "Well, he's cute. Seems like a decent enough guy."

"He's alright," Pati said. "Good at dishes. Terrible at biking."

There was a lull in their banter as both women watched the silhouettes dancing in the firelight—bare feet, waves of laughter, beer bottles raised like offerings to the stars.

Rachel turned toward her, voice lowered. "It's getting close, Pati."

Pati took a slow sip of her beer, considering that. "I know."

"You scared?"

Pati rolled the bottle between her hands. "Nah."

"Really?"

Pati glanced sideways at her. "I don't fit the profile. Not unless the guy suddenly develops a taste for short-haired brown-eyed bartenders with a mild nicotine addiction and a criminally under-watered aloe plant."

Rachel raised an eyebrow. "The rumor is they've all had blue eyes."

"And long brown hair," Pati added. "Girl-next-door types. Sweet. Sad-eyed. Definitely not me."

Rachel made a skeptical noise. "That's a hell of a gamble to place on a rumor."

Pati shrugged. "If I'm wrong, I'll haunt you just to say I told you so."

"Comforting."

They stood in silence again, the sound of the waves just barely audible beneath the hum of the party.

Finally, Pati said, "If my sister were down here, I'd tell her to watch her back."

Rachel raised a brow. "Clara?"

"Yeah. She's the type. Blue eyes, long brown hair. If only the rumor was that all these victims also had a permanent aura of superiority."

"Didn't she hate the Keys?"

"Hated me living in the Keys. Thought I was wasting my potential by pouring shots and learning all the Jimmy Buffett deep cuts. She'd rather die than be away from a major city."

Rachel shook her head. "How is she your sister?"

"DNA roulette," Pati said, raising her bottle again.

Rachel paused. "You think Michel's involved, don't you?"

Pati didn't answer right away. The breeze kicked up a bit, carrying with it the salty tang of the ocean and the faintest whiff of something sweet—maybe someone was lighting up behind them.

"I don't know," she said finally. "But something about him gives me the creeps. He's too... deliberate. You ever meet someone who feels like they're trying to play a part? Like, if you looked too hard, you'd see the seams?"

"Tourist pretending to be local?"

"No. More like... alien pretending to be human."

Rachel laughed, then realized Pati wasn't joking. "Seriously?"

Pati stared ahead, eyes narrowed. "He played 'La Vie en Rose' on the jukebox."

"That's not a crime."

"It was the way he did it. Like he'd done it a hundred times before in a hundred different bars. Like it meant something."

Rachel frowned. "You think it's a signature?"

"I don't know what I think," Pati said. "But I texted you when I saw him at the Parrot because something about him twisted in my gut. And when the cops say someone heard the killer speaking with a French accent, I don't know. It just... hits different now."

Rachel leaned on the railing, letting the weight of that hang in the air.

"I don't want to accuse someone based on an accent," Pati added quickly. "But I trust my instincts. And my instincts are telling me he's not just some moody loner on vacation."

Rachel took a long sip of her drink. "Have you told the cops?"

Pati shook her head. "I don't have anything real to give them. Just a bad feeling and a song. And the cops around here? They don't jump until someone's already in the water."

"So," Rachel sighed. "If he's after blue-eyed women with brown hair, do you think I'm at risk?"

Patti hadn't even thought about that. "Oh my god, Rachel, I'm so sorry; I didn't mean to imply—"

Rachel cut her off, laughing. "Pati, it's fine. The cops haven't even reported a motive like that. It's all hearsay, and I'm not going to get worked up over island rumors."

They stood there a while longer, saying nothing. The wind picked up again, ruffling the short tufts of hair at the nape of Pati's neck.

Rachel finally nudged her with a shoulder. "You need a drink refill or a change of subject?"

"Both," Pati said. "Preferably in reverse order."

Rachel grinned. "Let's go find your delinquent houseguest. Last I saw, he was flirting with Tia or doing a keg stand. Possibly both."

Pati shook her head. "God help me."

They turned and walked back toward the noise, the firelight casting tall, stretching shadows behind them— two women moving forward through the darkness, with just enough light to see each other's faces.

CHAPTER 6
EMBERS AND ECHOES

The bonfire had burned down to a wide, pulsing glow, more ember than flame now. Sparks floated skyward like lazy fireflies, and someone had swapped the Bluetooth speaker's country playlist for something slower—it sounded like indie folk, but Pati wasn't sure what the song was. Either way, it fit. The kind of music that made people lean in closer, speak a little softer.

Pati stood at the edge of the ring, watching a group pass a guitar back and forth like a campfire confessional. She had another beer in her hand—someone handed it to her, she wasn't sure who. The bottle was warm, and she didn't particularly want it, but holding it gave her something to do.

Rachel was still beside her for now, arms crossed, lips curled in a half-smile as she observed a girl in a pirate hat trying to do a handstand.

"Do you ever feel like this town is just... a loop?" Rachel asked suddenly.

Pati blinked. "What do you mean?"

Rachel shrugged. "Like, same faces, same places, different excuses to drink. Like we're all just orbiting each other until someone breaks the pattern."

Pati gave her a sidelong glance. "That's... existential for someone holding a rum punch in a can."

"I'm evolving." Rachel tipped her cup in salute and wandered off toward the drink table.

Pati watched her go. The crowd was shifting now—people drifting in waves, conversations splintering and reforming. A conga line of half-sober twenty-somethings snaked past her, whooping into the night like it owed them something.

Across the fire, she spotted a familiar face: Malik, a dive boat captain she hadn't seen in months. He was tall and rangy, with a laugh that could crack open a silent room. Pati used to run into him at karaoke nights, back when she still felt like singing badly into a mic without apology.

"Malik!" she called, waving.

He looked up, grinned. "Well, if it isn't the queen of gin and eye rolls."

They embraced like old co-conspirators, arms slung casually around each other's shoulders.

"Where the hell have you been?" Pati asked.

"Charters. Costa Rica. Then back here with a busted prop and too many stories. You still making magic at the Parrot?"

"Something like that."

They chatted for a while—easy, nostalgic banter. Malik had the kind of energy that made it feel like no time had passed at all. But eventually, the rhythm of the party pulled him away too. A new face caught his eye, and soon he was off again, swept into another circle of voices and beer cans and salt-slick laughter.

Pati found herself alone again, the party growing denser in some places and thinner in others. She turned to look for Danny. She spotted him near the far end of the fire circle, sitting in the sand with a group she didn't recognize by name but knew by sight—boat people, maybe. One guy had a leather vest over no shirt. A woman beside him wore a sequined headband and no shoes. Danny looked content, cross-legged in the sand, nursing a beer and nodding along to something they were saying.

He caught her eye, raised his drink in a lazy toast. She returned it, but didn't go over. He looked fine. Happy, even.

Pati drifted in the other direction, toward the darker edge of the beach, where the firelight didn't quite reach. The air cooled just slightly the further she went, and the ocean's voice grew louder—a gentle roar that smoothed the night's frayed edges.

A couple made out aggressively on a blanket under a palm tree. A trio of friends kicked a half-deflated volleyball around with more enthusiasm than coordination. Pati walked past them, letting the beach unfold before her like a quiet invitation. She wasn't sure what she was looking for. Maybe just space. Maybe something to help her make sense of the unease still buzzing beneath her skin. Maybe nothing at all.

The music behind her softened further. Someone was playing a melancholy acoustic tune now, the kind you only hear at beach parties or breakups. Pati let her feet guide her. She moved past the last glow of firelight and into the dark. Her sandals sank slightly with each step, grit collecting at her heels. The shoreline stretched like something forgotten—driftwood and seaweed scattered like old bones, and the mangroves casting long, crooked shadows.

She had just started to think about turning back when she spotted a figure ahead. A man, crouched near the edge of the water, sifting through something in the sand.

For a beat, she thought about veering away, pretending not to notice. But then he stood—and the light from the moon caught his profile just enough.

Michel. *Of course.*

He turned as if he sensed her, not startled—just aware.

"Bonsoir," he said, voice calm as the tide.

Pati slowed her steps. "Hey," she replied, keeping her voice level.

Michel smiled faintly. "I didn't expect company out here."

"Neither did I."

He glanced down at the ground again, then back up at her. "You walk the beach at night often?"

She didn't answer. Instead, she moved a little closer and saw what he was looking at—small stones, tangled threads of seaweed, a few shells, most broken.

"You collecting something?" she asked.

"Just looking," he said. "Sometimes I find things worth keeping."

Pati looked down. "Not a lot of seashells on this island. Tourists always think there will be."

"Yes, I've noticed," he said. "But if you're patient, sometimes something washes up. A bit of coral. A polished bit of glass. A coin."

"You expecting treasure?"

Michel smiled without looking at her. "No. But I like the idea that the sea leaves gifts behind. Even the smallest ones."

He picked up a smooth black stone, turned it over in his hand like it might tell him something, then slipped it into his pocket.

Pati watched him carefully. There was nothing overtly strange about what he was doing. Plenty of people collected beach junk. But there was something in the way he moved—methodical, quiet, like he was performing a ritual instead of a hobby.

"What do you do with the stuff?" she asked.

He looked up again. "Sometimes I keep it. Sometimes I give it away. I promised my nephew I'd bring him something from my travels. Something no one else would think to find."

Pati crossed her arms. "How old's your nephew?"

"Seven," he said. "Curious. Always asking questions. Wants to be a marine biologist, at least this month."

She tried to picture Michel talking to a kid—kneeling to show him a shell, explaining currents and coral formations with that same eerie calm. It didn't sit right. It was too composed. Too... prepared.

"You here alone?" she asked.

He tilted his head. "I am."

"No family visiting? No friends meeting you here?"

"No," he said, then smiled, faint and lopsided. "I like the solitude."

Pati didn't answer. A wave rolled in, closer than the last, licking at the edges of his shoes. He didn't move. Just let the water pass over and recede.

She nodded slowly, then looked back toward the glow of the bonfire, now just a warm smudge in the distance. "I should get back. Lost track of my friends."

Michel didn't follow her gaze. Just crouched again, brushing his fingers along the wet sand. "Of course. It was nice to see you again, Pati."

She turned without replying and started walking. Her footsteps were quicker this time, crunching over rock fragments and salt-dried seaweed. After a few yards, she glanced over her shoulder. Michel was still there, kneeling in the sand. His posture was almost reverent. Like he was listening for something only he could hear. Pati kept walking.

The embers of the bonfire grew closer and Michel faded behind her. About halfway back, Pati stopped. She heard something. Faint. Off-key.

Someone was humming. She recognized it. That damn song Michel had played in the bar: "La Vie en

Rose." She froze. Just for a second. Then she walked faster, heart climbing into her throat.

Pati's legs moved faster than her thoughts as she made her way back toward the firelight. The soft thrum of the party returned slowly, voices and laughter reentering her ears like static clearing on a radio. But the echo of Michel's humming still clung to her spine.

She shook it off. She scanned the clusters of people. The fire had burned low, now surrounded by groups of barefoot drinkers passing around bottles and sharing half-finished stories. Someone was playing a lazy tune on a guitar, but her eyes darted past it all, searching.

"Danny?" she called out. "Hey, Danny, you still here?"

No answer.

She spotted the musician Danny—beach-worn and cheerful, perched on a milk crate with his guitar—there were always multiple beach bums with guitars at these things. She jogged over.

"Hey—Danny?"

He looked up mid-strum. "Hey! Not me, the other one, right?"

"Yeah. You seen him?"

Musician Danny thought for a second, brushing a hand over his curls. "Last I saw, he was with Tia. They were at the folding table, playing beer pong. Tia was winning. He was losing graciously."

"When was that?"

He shrugged. "Half hour ago? Maybe more. Time's kind of flexible out here."

Pati nodded, already backing away. "Thanks."

She searched the drink table. No Tia. No Danny.

She circled once. Then twice. Checked near the water. Behind the fire. Called his name a few more times, quieter now. Gone.

She checked her phone. No messages.

Maybe he went to pee. Maybe he wandered off with Tia. Maybe he was chasing a breeze or a story or a memory. Still, the weight in her chest didn't like it.

She pulled her bike from where it leaned against a coconut palm, brushing sand from the seat. If she pedaled slow, he'd probably catch up.

But then the flashing lights cut through the trees. Blue and red strobes. Two beams at first, then more.

The crowd shifted like startled birds. Voices rising. Heads turning.

"Shit," someone said. "Cops."

Three officers strode down the path toward the beach, flashlights high, shoulders wide. Pati froze, one hand still on her bike. The party, once sprawling and fluid, suddenly snapped tight. People started moving—gathering bags, stuffing coolers, dumping drinks into the sand. The music cut off mid-chord.

"Time to go," someone muttered behind her.

The cops stepped onto the sand, boots crunching. One of them raised a hand.

"Evening. Bonfires aren't permitted on Higgs Beach. We're not handing out citations tonight, but y'all need to clear out. Take your trash with you and don't come back out here like this."

A chorus of yes sirs and sorrys. The crowd scattered like marbles on a tile floor. Laughter dimmed to mumbles, flip-flops slapped against damp sand, and coolers thumped closed in rushed apologies. The police presence wasn't heavy-handed, but it was enough—no one wanted to test how chill they really were.

Pati stayed close to her bike, half-shielded by a cluster of palms. She hadn't seen Danny or Tia. She hadn't seen Michel return either. The quiet wrongness of the night still tugged at her nerves. She watched as two officers broke off from the others, their flashlights carving harsh beams through the dark. They weren't moving with the same slow, steady rhythm anymore. Now, they were scanning—really scanning—eyes cutting across the sand, the brush, the edge of the tree line. Were they making sure no one stayed behind? Trying to catch someone from the party on a littering charge if they found trash?

Pati followed their movement with her eyes.

They were heading toward the way she'd just come from. The darker patch of beach where she'd found Michel alone, whispering to the sand. Her pulse skipped.

One of the flashlights swept in a wide arc, bouncing off clumps of grass, low shrubs, driftwood. Then it stopped. So did the cop holding it.

The second officer stepped forward. The beams of both lights converged in the grass, illuminating something pale. Not quite white. More like the underside of a seashell. Or skin.

"Shit," one of them muttered.

The first officer raised a hand. "Call it in."

A crackle of radio followed. Words too muffled for Pati to catch.

Around her, the dispersing crowd slowed again—uncertainty spreading like fog.

Someone whispered, "What are they looking at?"

"Did someone get arrested?"

Pati didn't move. Her fingers gripped the handlebars, cold and wet from the ocean air. More lights converged. One of the officers moved carefully through the grass, stepping over a tangle of dune vine and a piece of driftwood.

Then she heard it. Clear this time.

"We've got a body."

Everything stopped. A few people gasped. A girl dropped her solo cup in the sand. Pati didn't breathe. She was suddenly aware of every sound—the high click of a flashlight's button, the rustle of someone backing away too quickly, the thin hum of blood in her ears. She looked again toward the grass. From where she was, she couldn't see much of anything—just a circle of flashlight beams stabbing into the overgrowth. She caught a glimpse of something pale, maybe fabric, maybe not. But the way the cops moved—tight, tense, controlled—told her everything she needed to know.

Whoever it was, they weren't breathing. She shivered, sweat cooling fast on her skin. People were leaving faster now, some walking quickly, others whispering, a few pulling friends away by the arm. Pati stood rooted for a moment longer. The night was suddenly too quiet, too humid, too full. She craned her neck, but she couldn't see the body. Despite the humidity, she has goose bumps; she couldn't shake the feeling she might've spoken to the killer an hour ago. Or worse—that he might've been watching the party the entire time, waiting to strike.

CHAPTER 7
WHAT FOLLOWS YOU HOME

Pati pedaled like her life depended on it. The bike wobbled a little as she turned off White Street, sand grinding beneath the tires, the occasional pebble spitting out from under her tread. Her legs were jelly and overworked, but she didn't stop. Not even when her calves cramped or when the wind slapped her hair into her mouth.

She was more drunk than she wanted to admit and entirely more sober than she wanted to be. The air was hot and thick, clinging to her like an unwanted hand. Every rustle in the hedges felt pointed. Every flickering porch light was a warning. Her body buzzed with alcohol and fear, a sour combination that made the world tilt sideways every few blocks.

She turned onto her street too fast, the tires skidding slightly. "Shit," she muttered, steadying herself. Her front wheel clipped a curb and jolted her forward, but she gritted her teeth and kept going. All she could think was: Get home. Get inside. Lock the door.

A cat darted across the road in front of her, a gray blur with glowing eyes. Pati yelped and swerved, narrowly missing it, her heart banging like a drumline in her chest.

"Goddammit, Hemingway cats," she hissed through clenched teeth. She pedaled harder. Her thighs burned. Sweat dripped from the tip of her nose.

And then—CRASH. A sudden thud and clatter from her right made her scream. She swerved again and nearly toppled off her bike. For a terrifying second, she was sure someone had come out of the bushes. Some shadowy shape ready to grab her and—

But no. Just an iguana. The green bastard had launched itself off a wooden fence and landed directly onto a metal trash can, sending the lid skittering into the street like a flying saucer.

"Jesus!" she shouted, voice cracking with adrenaline. "Seriously?"

The iguana didn't apologize. It flicked its tail, looking more annoyed than she was, then skittered off into the shadows.

Pati pressed a hand to her chest, trying to calm her breath. Her heart felt like it was trying to punch its way out of her ribs.

"This island," she muttered, voice shaking. "This island is trying to kill me."

She kept riding. Past a sleepy Airbnb with a flickering porch light. Past an overgrown garden where wind chimes clanged out of rhythm. Past the corner store with its ghostly, humming freezer units. All of it looked wrong in the dark. Too quiet. Too sharp-edged. As if the entire neighborhood was holding its breath.

Her own breath didn't come easy either.

The body.

The cops.

Michel on the beach, humming that damn song like it was a lullaby meant to seduce the ocean itself.

She turned onto her block. Home came into view—just a squat little house with chipped paint and a hibiscus bush leaning too far into the driveway. But it had never looked better. She nearly cried when she saw the porch light was still on.

She didn't even lock the bike properly—just dropped it onto the front step and fumbled with her keys. Her hands were shaking so badly it took three tries to get the right one in the lock. When the deadbolt finally turned, she shoved the door open and stumbled inside.

She didn't breathe until it clicked shut behind her.

Home. The air inside was cooler—slightly. The ceiling fan turned in lazy loops, barely moving the heavy heat that had settled since sunset. Everything smelled faintly like coconut oil, sea salt, and the incense she'd burned earlier that week and never fully aired out.

She leaned against the door and exhaled. And then, suddenly, she was furious. Not at the body. Not even at Michel. At the night itself. At her own fear. At the sick pit sitting in her gut like a swallowed stone. At the fact that she was drunk and alone and had no idea where the hell Danny was.

"Please be here," she said under her breath, pushing off from the door. "Please tell me you're passed out watching some conspiracy doc on YouTube."

She kicked off her sandals, padding barefoot across the floor, every shadow feeling too long. But the house was quiet. Too quiet. And Danny was nowhere in sight.

Pati checked every room—quick glances, lights flicked on and off, her heart thudding a little harder with each empty corner. Danny wasn't there. The bathroom light was off. The kitchen untouched. His crusty water bottle from the porch was still on the counter, but his backpack was gone.

She stood in the middle of the living room, bare feet planted on cool tile, and tried to quiet her thoughts. He probably just kept partying. Maybe he'd gone off with Tia or someone else. Maybe he'd crashed on someone's boat.

Still, something in her gut twisted. But not the same fear as before. Not the creeping, bone-deep unease she'd felt with Michel. This was smaller, more familiar. Concern wrapped in irritation.

"He's fine," she muttered aloud. "He's a grown man. He's not… the type."

The type. Young. Pretty. Alone. Blue eyes. Long brown hair.

Danny was none of those. Plus he knew where she hid the spare key. He'd be fine.

She dragged herself into the bathroom and stripped off her clothes, tossing them into the laundry hamper like she was shedding the whole night along with them. The water took forever to warm, then came out too hot, scalding her neck and shoulders before settling into a soothing burn.

She stood under it for a long time. Let the steam fill the space. Let the salt and sand and sweat slide away. Let the pounding in her head dull to a low throb. She couldn't stop thinking about the body.

What if it wasn't random? What if it was one of the girls from the party? What if he'd followed someone?

She closed her eyes, leaned into the tile wall. The coolness felt good against her temple.

But then—Click.

The front door.

Pati's eyes snapped open.

Footsteps. The creak of the old wood near the couch. The unmistakable presence of someone entering her house.

"Danny?" she called, voice high and tight. "Is that you?"

No answer.

Her stomach dropped.

She shut off the water, heart hammering, and yanked the towel from the hook. Sloppily wrapping it around her body, she dripped water all over the tile as she stepped out. She grabbed her phone from the counter, screen slick with steam and shaking hands.

"Danny," she called again, louder this time. "Seriously, not funny."

Still nothing.

She cracked the door and peeked down the hallway, every inch of her tense.

And then—just around the corner—she saw him.

Face-down on the couch, legs sprawled out like a crime scene, one arm dangling off the side, and a half-empty bottle of red wine tipped dangerously in his hand. A dark stain was spreading across her favorite throw rug.

Pati's fear flipped instantly to fury.

"Are you kidding me?"

She stormed over, tugging the bottle from his fingers. "Since when do you drink wine?" she muttered. "You must've gotten really messed up."

Danny let out a snort but didn't stir. Fully out. Snoring into her throw pillow.

She clutched the wine bottle like it had personally betrayed her and stared down at the spreading stain.

"Great," she snapped. "Just great."

She grabbed a towel from the laundry basket and started blotting the rug. Not rubbing—never rub, she could hear her mother's voice say. But it was dark red, and the fibers were already soaked.

She muttered curses under her breath the entire time. By the time she'd dabbed most of it up and tossed the towel into the laundry pile, the anger had cooled into weary resignation. Pati looked back at Danny, still face-down and useless, and sighed.

"I hope you at least had a good night," she mumbled.

She turned out the light, left him snoring in the living room, and padded into her bedroom. The towel she'd been wearing dropped unceremoniously onto the floor.

Sleep. Just a few hours. Then maybe this wouldn't feel so sharp.

But even as she lay down, eyes closed, the edges of the night still clung to her—fragments of the beach, the cops, the flashlight beams, the pale thing in the grass. And somewhere beneath it all, a melody still hummed at the edge of her thoughts, as if it had followed her home.

Pati lay flat on her back, eyes wide open, staring at the ceiling. She hadn't bothered turning off the bedside lamp. The low, amber glow barely pushed back the dark corners of her room, but it felt safer than being alone with the shadows. She told herself she wasn't afraid of the dark— just what her mind might do in it.

Outside, wind scraped against the siding. A palm branch tapped the roof like it was trying to be let in. She shifted under the sheet. Too hot. She kicked it off. Too cold. She pulled it back. Her head ached in that deep, poisoned way—half from booze, half from adrenaline, like her body hadn't caught up with the night yet.

The image wouldn't leave her. The circle of flashlights. The way the cops moved—calculated, quiet, serious in that way only real death demanded. They hadn't said who it was. They hadn't said how it was. Was it someone from the party?

She thought of the girls she'd seen earlier. The one with the pirate hat doing handstands. The ones playing beer pong. Tia from MoonDog—although she didn't fit the killer's M.O. either with her light brown skin. That new girl Rachel had been talking to—Heather? Holly? She couldn't remember now. Couldn't pin down a single face clearly.

Could Michel have lured someone away? Wouldn't someone have noticed?

Pati squeezed her eyes shut. The beach flickered behind her lids like film reels on loop—Michel crouched in the sand, brushing it like it whispered secrets. That glassy tone in his voice. The smooth black stone in his hand. And then that humming.

She could still hear it if she stayed too still. But maybe the body wasn't his doing. Maybe someone got too drunk, wandered too far. Maybe they tripped on the rocks or passed out and never woke up. It happened. Rare, but it happened.

But that's not how the cops acted. They weren't scrambling. They weren't doing CPR. They were calling it in, eyes steady, movements practiced. There was no urgency. Just inevitability.

And had one of them actually said the word body?

She couldn't remember exactly. Her mind filled in the blank anyway. Was the body posed? Like the others? No one said that out loud. Not tonight. Not yet.

But something about the way they stood around it—

the way they didn't rush—made her think they'd seen something like it before. Pati rolled onto her side, curling inward. She hated this part. The not-knowing. The endless, tightening swirl of what-ifs. The invisible weight of danger in every silence.

And through it all, she could hear Danny snoring down the hall, undisturbed and wine-logged. Safe. At least he was safe. For now.

She flipped her pillow, chased the cool side like it could fix everything. It didn't.

The night stretched long and breathless. A heavy thing with no end. And Pati lay awake inside it, waiting for morning like it might bring answers.

CHAPTER 8
COFFEE, CROISSANTS, AND CORPSES

The first light of morning slipped through the slats of the blinds, streaking Pati's bedroom wall with pale gold. She hadn't slept. Not really. Her body had gone through the motions—blankets pulled tight, limbs tangled, pillow flipped half a dozen times—but rest had been impossible. Her brain had refused to shut off, skipping from memory to dread like a scratched record stuck in all the wrong places.

When she finally gave up pretending to sleep, it was barely 6:30 a.m. The fan overhead clicked with every rotation, a mechanical reminder that she hadn't left the island, hadn't outrun the night, hadn't solved a damn thing. She sat up slowly, rubbing her face with both hands. Her mouth tasted like regret and old gin.

The apartment was silent except for the distant whoosh of a passing car and the occasional groan of the fridge cycling on. She pulled on a loose T-shirt and some soft, salt-stiffened shorts before stepping barefoot into the hall.

Danny hadn't moved. He was still sprawled face-down on the couch, one sock half-off, one arm dangling like a forgotten puppet. The empty wine bottle was in the sink—thankfully—but the dark stain on her rug remained, a ghost of last night's chaos.

"Jesus," she muttered, crouching beside him.

She hesitated, unsure if she should wake him, shake him, or just let him rot in the wine-soaked cocoon he'd made for himself. Ultimately, she stood up and let him be. He clearly had a night. Who knows how he even got home? Maybe he walked. Maybe he got a ride.

Maybe he sleep-teleported. Whatever. She wasn't in the mood to unravel that mystery yet. She glanced out the window. Sunlight was warming the tops of the palms and beginning to bleach the sky. Her stomach churned— equal parts hunger, nerves, and hangover.

Definitely not pedaling anywhere today. She grabbed her keys and slid on an old pair of Vans, shuffling out the door to the carport. Her electric moped sat there like a little green miracle. She thumbed the power button, slung her tote bag over one shoulder, and pulled on her helmet. The ride down White Street was smooth and quiet. Even the town felt hungover—quiet sidewalks, shuttered windows, a light breeze tugging at the corners of old flyers stapled to telephone poles.

When she reached MoonDog Café, it was just opening. A bell jingled softly overhead as she stepped inside. And there, behind the counter, wiping down a pastry case with a sunflower-yellow cloth, was Casey.

Pati blinked. "You still work here?"

Casey looked up and grinned. "Surprise."

"I thought you were a full-time artist now."

"I am," Casey said, crumpling the cloth and tossing it under the counter. "Mostly. But I still work here one day a week. I couldn't leave Des and Tia hanging. And who doesn't love the end-of-day employee pastry grab?"

Pati smirked, stepping up to the register. "You got that almond croissant today?"

"Not yet, but if you bribe me with gossip, I'll save you one."

"You want gossip?" Pati leaned on the counter. "Last night turned into a mess. Party at Higgs got broken up by the cops."

Casey raised an eyebrow. "Really? We left early—me and Phillip. I had to work this morning, obviously."

"You missed the drama, then." Pati sighed. "People were scattering. Cops didn't want to write tickets—just wanted everyone gone."

"Well," Casey said, tapping something into the tablet screen, "they must've been in a good mood. Higgs can be a mess on Saturday nights."

Pati rubbed her temples. "Yeah, but…" her stomach churned with the thought of the body. "I'll tell you in a sec—I need food first. I'm barely human right now."

"Respect." Casey nodded toward the kitchen. "Whatcha want? I'll put it in to Luc before the early bird regulars show up."

"Breakfast tacos, please. And a black coffee." Pati smiled.

"Go grab a seat. I'll bring it out." Casey said, pouring a mug of black coffee and sliding it across the counter.

Pati gave her a grateful half-salute and dropped into a corner table near the window. The air conditioning was doing its best, humming softly, and the smell of espresso and sugar clung to the air like a promise. She slumped back against the seat, eyes drifting to the quiet street outside. It all looked so normal. But nothing about the night before felt normal.

She glanced back toward the counter. Casey was chatting with someone who'd just come in—a guy in board shorts with a man bun and too many tattoos. Pati closed her eyes for a moment, letting the room steady around her.

When she opened them again, she caught Casey watching her from the espresso machine. There was something kind in her gaze. Steady. Pati appreciated it more than she could say. She sat back and sipped her coffee, waiting for breakfast, knowing she was going to have to talk about the body soon. And not at all sure she was ready.

Casey returned with Pati's food, the wax paper warm and slightly damp beneath the weight of three breakfast tacos. Each one was a perfect little mess of scrambled eggs nestled inside soft corn tortillas, topped with crumbles of queso fresco, creamy avocado slices, a bright spoonful of pico de gallo, and a vibrant green drizzle of chimichurri that smelled like fresh herbs and garlic heaven.

She set it down with a proud smile. "Hangover armor. You're welcome."

Pati leaned forward, inhaling. "You're a lifesaver."

"Tell me something I don't know," Casey said, wiping her hands on her apron as the door chimed behind her.

The sunlight poured in like liquid heat, and with it came Tia—oversized sunglasses, yesterday's eyeliner smudged like intentional art, and a half-open linen shirt over a bikini top. She looked like she'd been rolled out of the ocean and straight into the day.

"Praise be," she said, heading for the counter. "I need grease, bubbles, and salt. Immediately."

"Morning, Tia," Casey called. "Want your usual hangover kit?"

"Mimosa, egg and cheese croissant with avocado, and a hashbrown if you love me."

"I love you medium," Casey said, already ringing her up.

"Rude." Tia turned and spotted Pati. "Oh thank God. A fellow survivor."

Pati raised a taco in greeting. "Barely."

Tia slid into the seat across from her with a sigh that sounded like it had been aging in a barrel since midnight. She plucked her sunglasses off and rubbed her temples. "I feel like I got hit by a wave of bad decisions."

"You kinda did," Casey said as she brought over the mimosa and leaned on the edge of the table. "You don't remember insisting we all call you 'Captain Tequila' and trying to lead a pirate-themed conga line all before 11 p.m.?"

"I do now," Tia said, grimacing. "Was it awesome?"

"Moderately," Casey said.

Pati took a bite of her taco and spoke with her mouth half full. "Were you still there when the cops showed up?"

"Barely," Tia said, sipping her drink. "I saw the lights and bolted. Didn't even say bye. Just grabbed my shoes and ran like I was avoiding student loans."

"You didn't hear what happened?" Pati asked carefully.

Tia looked up, suspicious. "No… why? What happened?"

Pati lowered her taco. "They found a body."

Silence settled like a fog.

"A body?" Casey repeated, her voice sharper now.

Tia blinked. "Wait—what?"

"Down past the edge of the party. In the brush," Pati said, her voice low. "Cops were calm about it. Too calm."

"Oh my god," Casey whispered.

"I didn't see anything," Tia said quickly. "No one said anything—there was no panic. Just—get out of here, cops are coming, grab your beer and bounce."

Casey sat down slowly. "Was it someone from the party?"

"No idea," Pati said. "They didn't say. Just flashlight beams and a bunch of 'back up, ma'am' vibes."

They all went quiet for a beat. Pati pushed at her avocado with her fork.

"You think it was… him?" Casey asked finally, not naming Michel out loud. "You know; the weird guy with the French accent at the Parrot the other day? And no, not my weird guy with the French accent," she added with a light laugh, trying to lighten the mood with the coincidence that she happened to be dating a brooding tattoo artist born and raised in Nice, France.

Pati forced a smile and shrugged one shoulder. "That's what's strange," Pati relented. "Weird guy was out there. Alone. On the beach. Doing some weird little beachcomber ritual. Said he was looking for treasures. I saw him like fifteen-twenty minutes before the cops showed up."

"That guy gives me serial killer vibes," Casey said. "Always so polite. Like Stepford polite."

"I didn't think much of it until I saw the cops," Pati said. "But now… I don't know. Could've been an accident too, I guess."

"I don't like that either," Tia muttered, tearing off a piece of croissant. "Some poor drunk girl stumbles too far, hits her head on dried up coral, and that's it? God."

The conversation hung there, heavy with implications. It was speculation, of course, but gossip traveled fast on the Coconut Telegraph, or so the islanders called it. The café had its usual sounds—the hiss of the espresso machine, the low hum of indie music, a distant blender—but it all felt muffled now.

Pati polished off the last bite of her last taco and wiped her hands with a napkin.

"Well," she said, standing, "I'm gonna head up the street. The Parrot's closed, but I've got the key."

"You sure you're okay?" Casey asked.

Pati managed a tired smile. "Not even a little."

Tia gave a mock toast with her mimosa. "To surviving."

Pati clinked her coffee mug against it. "Barely."

She paid at the counter and slipped back out into the sun. The humidity hit her like a damp slap, but she welcomed it. The Green Parrot wouldn't be open yet, but at least it was familiar. At least it was hers.

And she needed that right now. Something real. Something solid. Something that didn't hum a haunting tune under its breath when no one was watching.

CHAPTER 9
BEFORE THE BAR OPENS

The Green Parrot was a different creature in the early hours. Without the music, the bodies, the booze, it was just bones—wood and dust and a smell that lingered no matter how many times you mopped. Pati unlocked the front door with her own key and pushed it open with her hip, the swollen frame groaning like always. Inside, the air was thick and still. A thin line of morning light sliced through the half-closed blinds, landing in a puddle of gold across the worn floor.

She flipped on the lights above the bar but left the rest of the place in its quiet. No need to startle the ghosts. The hum of the fridge kicked on. The ice machine clattered to life. She made a pot of coffee in the back—the strong stuff meant to burn off hangovers and keep shaky hands steady through morning prep—and poured herself the first cup. It steamed in her hands as she sat at the bar, elbows on the wood, eyes on nothing.

This was her favorite time of day here, if she had to pick one. Before the voices, before the jukebox, before the regulars came in talking about boats and breakups and which restaurant was understaffed this week. She liked the hush. The stillness. Just her and the bar and the coffee and the ghosts.

She checked her phone. 9:15 a.m.

Technically, the opener should be here by now. But no one ever came right at nine. Everyone was always ten minutes late. Or fifteen. Sometimes more. Especially after nights like the one they'd just had. Bonfires on Higgs Beach, cheap rum, sweaty dancing in the sand. Most of the island had been there at some point. A lot of Parrot folks too.

So when the clock crept toward 9:30, Pati didn't panic. Not yet. She set down her empty cup and started slicing citrus. Limes. Lemons. Oranges. The rhythm was familiar, soothing. Muscle memory. The paring knife moved confidently through the fruit, wedges dropping into the plastic caddy with soft thuds. But still—no opener.

She rinsed her hands, wiped them on a towel slung over her shoulder, and crossed to the staff binder tucked beneath the point-of-sale terminal. Flipping it open, she scanned the schedule. Her stomach did a small, annoyed twist when she saw the name written in blue pen next to today's date. Rachel.

"Shit," she muttered.

Rachel was steady. Solid. Showed up even when she had the flu, even when she was hungover, even when her dog chewed up her only pair of non-slip shoes. If she wasn't here by now, something was off.

Pati stared at the page for a few more seconds. She could still picture Rachel laughing last night, drink in hand, ash from a joint curling between her fingers. Her cheeks flushed with heat and rum and the wild edge of a beach party too big to control.

"Damn it, Rachel," she said aloud this time.

Still, she didn't reach for her phone. Not yet. She wasn't her boss. She wasn't going to be the nag who texted just because someone rolled in late once after a big night. She wasn't her mom. Besides, it wasn't like she had anywhere else to be.

She sighed and went back to the bar. If she was stuck here, she might as well get the damn place ready. She filled the ice bins, refreshed the napkin stacks, popped the tops off the mixers and restocked the speed rack. She was halfway through replacing the backup tequila when she realized just how quiet it still was.

She paused, bottle in hand.

The Parrot felt heavier today. Not in the air—though the humidity was already pushing in—but in the walls. Like the bones of the place were waiting for something she hadn't caught wind of yet. She shook the thought off. Blame it on the hangover. Blame it on the news. Blame it on the damn jukebox.

She poured herself a second cup of coffee and leaned on the bar, watching the sunlight stretch across the floor, inching toward the jukebox like it wanted to press play on something it couldn't name.

The clock read 9:42. Rachel still hadn't walked in. And Pati still hadn't texted. Because maybe she didn't want anyone else here yet. Maybe she wanted to sit with her coffee and her uneasy thoughts and try to make sense of the island she used to know.

She reached behind the bar for a clean glass. Something in her gut was shifting now. The kind of twist she couldn't ignore. A warning, maybe. Or maybe just the last calm breath before the storm.

She sipped the coffee, watching the door. And then it creaked.

"It's about time," she called out, not bothering to mask the edge in her voice. "I was starting to think you'd died in the sand, Rachel."

No answer. Just the faint scuff of soles on the floorboards, slow and deliberate. Pati straightened, rag still in hand, and turned toward the sound.

Michel.

She froze for half a breath—not out of fear exactly, but out of the instant, cold-bellied recognition that something was wrong with the shape of the day. Like a sour note in a familiar song.

He smiled when he saw her. "I didn't realize you were expecting me," he said, voice all silk and syrup.

Her jaw tightened. "I wasn't. The bar's not open yet."

He stepped closer anyway, hands clasped loosely in front of him like he had all the time in the world. "That's a shame. I was hoping to start my morning with a glass of wine. Something red."

Pati raised an eyebrow. "You'll have to wait. I thought you were our opening bartender coming in late. But since you're not, you'll need to step outside until we're open."

She held his gaze, not blinking.

Michel didn't budge. If anything, his smile grew more amused. "I understand. Of course. But it's just us in here, no?"

"That's right," she said. "And it's not a party."

Still he didn't move. She could feel her pulse starting to climb, a flutter in her throat she didn't like. Pati wasn't afraid of much—not drunk assholes, not fights, not cops—but this man made her skin hum in the wrong key. Too still. Too calm. Like he was acting out something he'd rehearsed.

"I'm not serving you," she said, firm now. "We don't open until ten."

That was a lie and they both knew it. She'd served regulars before opening plenty of times. Rachel had once started pouring beers at 9:15 when the power went out and the old-timers wandered in dripping with sweat. Hell, Pati had handed off whiskey to her neighbor more than once just to help him kill a hangover early. But that was family. Island people. Not this tourist with a too-smooth accent and a way of looking at you like he already knew how the conversation would end.

Michel didn't argue. He simply turned away, and for a moment, relief washed over her. She thought he was going to leave. Good. She didn't want to deal with him. Didn't want to keep staring down this feeling in her chest like static before a storm. But instead of heading to the door, he veered toward the jukebox in the corner.

Pati's blood went cold. He pressed the power button, and the machine let out its familiar electronic groan, followed by two distinct mechanical clicks. She didn't need to wait for the song. She already knew what it would be.

Sure enough, the opening chords slid out like an oily ghost. That song. That fucking song.

She gripped the bar so hard her knuckles turned white. Her jaw clenched. The jukebox cast a flickering light across the dark wood floor as Michel swayed along to the music, head cocked slightly, eyes half-lidded in what looked like pleasure.

He was dancing. Not quite to the beat—just to some rhythm inside himself. Something private. Something deeply unnerving.

Was he taunting her? Did he know she'd pegged him as a suspect? No. He couldn't know that. Could he?

Pati's heart thudded in her chest, not with fear this time, but with pure, unfiltered rage. Her instincts screamed at her to do something—yell, throw something, shove him out the door—but she knew better. Rage was only useful if you kept it sharp. Directed.

She reached beneath the bar and grabbed her phone from the shelf. There was one number saved under "Nate R. - FantasyFest Cop." He'd helped her break up a particularly ugly brawl a few years back. Stayed late to clean up the glass even though it wasn't in his job description. Gave her his number afterward "just in case." She hadn't used it since.

Pati stepped outside quietly, the heavy door falling shut behind her with a dull thud. The heat hit her like a slap. Already humid, already loud with the whir of scooters and a lawn mower a few streets over. But the air out here felt safer than inside.

She hit call. Two rings. Then: "Rusiek."

His voice was casual, still gravelly with sleep.

"Nate. It's Pati. Sorry to bother you."

"Wow. Having a problem this early at the Parrot?" he chuckled.

"Yeah," she said. "I think I might be sitting with a serial killer."

The silence on the other end of the line was immediate.

She went on. "He's been hanging around a lot lately. He came in before opening. Won't leave. He's polite but... weird. Persistent. Asked for wine. Turned on the jukebox...and he was at the beach last night where," Pati trailed off.

"You mean—?"

"Yeah. That one."

Nate exhaled. "You're sure?"

"I'm not sure of anything," she said. "Except that Rachel's supposed to be opening and she's not here. And this guy... Michel. He's off."

"Is he still there?"

"He is."

"Keep him there," Nate said. "Don't let him leave. I'll come over with the detective working the case."

"Okay."

"And Pati?"

"Yeah?"

"Be careful."

She hung up and stood for a moment on the cracked sidewalk, staring out at the empty street. Her hands were shaking, just slightly. Enough to notice.

Then she walked back inside.

The music was still playing. Michel was still dancing. And Pati—Pati was done pretending it was just another shitty day in paradise.

Michel had moved on to a new song—some dusty old B-side that hadn't seen daylight on that jukebox since the early 2000s. Maybe longer. The sound of it filled the space like a bad memory. He stood with his back to her, head bobbing gently, hands tucked into his pockets like he was waiting for a latte at a sidewalk café.

She cleared her throat. "It's ten," she said. "So I can officially serve you now."

Michel turned slowly, as if the music had to let go of him first. "Ah," he said with a smile. "Wonderful."

He moved back to the bar and took a seat with the ease of someone who'd done it a hundred times. Pati reached for the wine bottle she'd never wanted to open and poured a splash into a glass. She didn't ask if he wanted a full pour. She didn't care. She just wanted him seated, sipping, still.

She handed it to him. He held the glass delicately, like it might shatter if he breathed on it too hard.

"This is really is a nice place," he said.

Pati forced a nod, keeping her eyes on the glassware she began to polish. "Locals like it."

"And you?" he asked, taking a sip. "You must like it, too, no? You've worked here a long time, I imagine."

"Long enough," she said.

He smiled, sipping again. "Do you ever wonder what it would be like to just disappear? Start over somewhere else? Somewhere cold, maybe. Where nobody knows your name. I hear Nova Scotia is beautiful in the off-season."

Pati's stomach turned.

"Can't say I've thought about it," she replied. "This island's got claws."

Michel chuckled, a low, indulgent sound. "Yes. Yes, I suppose it does. I could see myself getting lost here if I didn't really love life up north."

She nodded, said nothing, and turned her attention to polishing the same glass she'd already wiped twice. Her eyes flicked to the clock. 10:07. Where the hell were they?

Michel seemed content to talk. She let him. Let the sound of his voice fill the air instead of the silence. He asked about the rum collection, about the history of the bar, about whether she thought hurricanes were going to get worse in the next decade. She answered in short, steady sentences. Her mind was only half on the words. The other half was praying—don't let anyone else walk in, don't let this place fill up, don't let anything happen before they get here. And then, finally, the door opened. She didn't flinch, didn't react, didn't let her breath escape.

Officer Nate Rusiek walked in first, his presence all worn denim and steady authority. Behind him came Detective Trent Morillo—taller, darker, eyes sharp like broken glass tucked in velvet. Neither was in uniform, but both had the weight of the law on their shoulders. Pati moved around the bar before they even fully stepped inside.

"Out back," she murmured, nodding toward the side hallway. They followed her into the narrow space near the mop sink, far enough from the jukebox that they couldn't be overheard.

"He's here. That's him," she said. "His name's Michel. He's been hanging around all week, always alone. Always asking weird questions. And he was at Higgs Beach last night. In the same direction of the beach they found that body."

Trent nodded. "You've done good. Just stay calm. We're gonna talk to him."

Pati narrowed her eyes slightly. "You both okay?"

"We're fine," Nate said, though his smile didn't reach his eyes. "It's just... not every day we walk into something like this. You know how small this island is."

"Yeah," she muttered. "I know. Speaking of small island—did you identify the body?"

Nate and Trent exchanged tense glances. Nate began to speak but Trent interrupted him.

"We unfortunately need multiple points of identification before we can release that information, and we are having someone close to her validate the identification this morning."

Pati nodded and took a deep breath. They stepped back into the main room together, and Pati slipped behind the bar. She grabbed a clean rag and another glass, keeping her hands moving even as her attention zeroed in on the three men. Nate and Trent approached the bar like they were just stopping in for a drink. Pati could see the act—laid-back postures, easy smiles—but she also saw the way their eyes tracked Michel's hands. The way they stayed out of arm's reach.

"Morning," Nate said. "Mind if we sit?"

Michel turned to face them, eyebrows lifting in surprise. "Of course not. Please."

Trent gestured toward the coffee pot behind the bar. "Could use some caffeine."

Pati poured two cups, wordlessly, and slid them over.

Michel raised his glass. "Cheers."

The conversation began like any other. Names, small talk, casual questions. Michel answered smoothly, his accent curling softly around his words. Pati kept her hands busy, wiping glasses that didn't need wiping, straightening napkin holders that were already perfect. But she was listening.

Trent shifted the tone just slightly. "You were at the beach last night, right?"

Michel nodded. "Yes, Higgs Beach. There was a bonfire. Quite a crowd."

"Big night," Nate agreed. "Did you stay late?"

Michel tilted his head. "Not too late. I left before midnight."

"You see anything unusual before you left?"

Michel blinked. "No. I did see police lights later, from a distance. Looked like they were breaking up the party."

"Down the beach from where the bonfire was?" Nate asked.

"Yes. Far enough I couldn't see what was going on. I assumed it was related to the party... you were there, no?" He looked at Pati.

She didn't flinch. Just shrugged. "For a while."

Trent leaned forward. "We're not asking about the party, though."

Michel sat back. His smile had faded. "Oh?"

"No," Trent said. "We're asking because a body was found. On that stretch of beach."

Michel's eyebrows rose, but not in shock. In offense. "You think I...?"

"We're not accusing anyone," Nate said. "We're just asking questions."

Michel's mouth pulled tight. "Of course. Of course. You must understand, this is... absurd. I don't know anything about a body. I was just there looking for washed up treasures."

Trent nodded slowly. "And on October fifth? Were you on Stock Island?"

Michel hesitated. "October fifth?"

"The night of the Stock Island murder."

Pati watched him closely now. His hands were still. His wine untouched. His face registered confusion, then a flicker of calculation.

"I was on a tour that night. One of those late-night haunted walks. There were two older tourists with me, a couple from Minnesota. I can give you the name of the company."

"Please do," Trent said.

Michel reached into his pocket and pulled out a slim wallet. From it, he retrieved a folded brochure and handed it over. "They stamp the dates for rebooking," he said. "I'm quite sure I was with them then."

"We'll follow up," Nate said. "In the meantime, would you mind coming with us to the station? Just to talk a little more."

Michel stared at them. He didn't move. Then, after a long pause, he smiled. "If it helps clear this up, of course."

He picked up his wine and drained it in one smooth gulp. Then he stood, adjusted the collar of his shirt, and nodded toward the door.

"Lead the way."

Trent and Nate flanked him as they exited, no cuffs,

no force. Just quiet steps and polite nods. Trent looked at Pati.

"You got any latex gloves back there?"

Pati's face scrunched in confusion but she grabbed the box and offered it to the detective. He pulled one out, snapped it onto his hand, and picked up the glass Michel had been drinking out of.

"Bill the department for the glass," he said.

The moment the door shut behind them, Pati's knees nearly buckled. She braced herself against the bar, the cold rag still clutched in her hand. She looked down and realized she'd broken the glass she'd been polishing—hairline cracks spiderwebbed through the base.

She tossed it in the bin and reached for a fresh one. It was going to be a long day.

CHAPTER 10
OFF THE SCHEDULE

Pati hadn't planned to be at the Green Parrot this long. Not today. Not after that kind of morning. But Rachel still hadn't shown up, and there was no one else around to take over. She wasn't technically on the schedule, but Key West didn't care much for technicalities. Not when it came to keeping bars open and tourists hydrated (or drunk).

She sighed and leaned against the back bar, letting her gaze drift toward the front windows. The sun outside was doing its best impression of a slow roast, casting long beams across the sticky floor. The overhead fan spun lazy circles above her, more for show than any actual airflow.

Rachel. What the hell.

Pati imagined her curled up on the couch, limbs tangled in an old blanket, totally passed out. Probably still in her clothes from the night before, mascara smudged halfway down her cheek. That wasn't like her—Rachel usually bounced back better than most—but still. Pati could picture it too clearly.

Maybe she and Danny had split that bottle of red, after all. Danny had definitely stumbled into Pati's place sometime after one. He scared the shit out of her, but she'd found him sprawled face down on her couch like a shipwrecked castaway. He hadn't even brought a blanket—just collapsed with his shoes still on and a faint whiff of salt and tequila clinging to him.

She smirked at the thought. Maybe they'd shared that wine, and Danny just brought the last swig home with him. The image brought a faint flicker of levity, but it didn't stick. Her mind kept circling back to Michel. To the way he moved. The way he talked. The way he played that song like it meant something. The memory made her jaw clench again. She shook it off, rolling her shoulders back as if she could shrug away the whole damn morning.

"Okay, fine," she muttered to herself. "Guess I'm clocked in now."

She pulled out the tip jar and set it in place, even though she doubted anyone would be walking in for a while. It wasn't just slow—it was quiet. Even the usual sounds of Duval Street traffic felt muffled, like the island was holding its breath. The Parrot was still empty. No music, no chatter, no clink of glasses. Just the hum of the fridge and the soft whirl of the ceiling fan above her head.

Rachel better have a hell of a story, Pati thought. Or a hangover so bad it comes with a doctor's note. She didn't want to be mad. Not really. Not if something had actually happened. But dammit, she was tired. And sore. And rattled in a way she couldn't quite name.

Still, she stayed. Because that's what you did when the island tilted sideways. You held the bar steady.

By noon, the bar still felt hollow. The Parrot usually pulsed by now—someone nursing a hangover at the end stool, someone else ordering their second mimosa before lunch, music rattling faintly from the jukebox whether anyone had asked for it or not. But today? It was silent. Not just quiet—silent. Like the place knew something Pati didn't.

Outside, the heat clung to the windows. Even the breeze seemed to have given up. The sidewalk looked deserted, and the normal clatter of scooters and chatter of early-day drinkers was conspicuously absent. Maybe it was the humidity. Maybe it was the news. Maybe the whole island was just hungover and pretending not to exist.

Pati didn't blame them. She wasn't exactly broadcasting welcoming energy herself.

The lights were dimmed. The music was off. The fans were spinning but slow, as if even they couldn't muster the usual gusto. The bar was fully stocked, but untouched. She hadn't even wiped down the tables again, which was usually the first thing she did when the place was empty. Her body moved on habit, but her heart wasn't in it. Her phone buzzed, the sudden vibration on the bar loud in the stillness. She snatched it up, pulse quickening. Maybe Rachel, finally explaining herself.

But it wasn't Rachel.

Danny: *Where you at?*

Pati exhaled, half annoyed, half relieved it was someone familiar. She tapped back a quick reply.

At the Parrot. Filling in because someone flaked.

The dots pulsed, then stilled. Then: *Lol. I'll come by. Gonna hitch a ride into old town. Need food anyway— grabbing a chocolate milk and sandwich at Fausto's. You want anything?*

Pati stared at the screen. She didn't know if she was hungry. Her stomach felt twisted in too many directions.

No thanks. Just get here.

She put her phone down and ran a hand through her hair, suddenly aware of how sticky her skin had gotten. She thought about stepping out for air but knew it wouldn't help. It was just as muggy outside—worse, maybe.

Danny showing up would at least give her something to focus on. A little noise. A little movement. Maybe even a laugh if they were lucky. She glanced again at the front door. Still closed. Still no Rachel. Where the hell was she?

Pati turned back toward the bar, flipping over a coaster she'd already flipped twice. It was going to be a long damn day. But for now, she'd just keep pretending the stillness wasn't pressing in too close. She poured herself a half shot of rum—just enough to sting the edge off—and waited for Danny to bring the outside world back in with him.

The door creaked open just after 1 p.m., and Danny stepped in like he was arriving late to brunch—not to a ghost town of a bar in the middle of a silent, sweltering Key West afternoon. He had a sandwich wrapped in wax paper clutched in one hand, a bottle of chocolate milk tucked under his arm, and his curls pulled back in a lazy, half-assed bun.

"God, it's hot," he said by way of greeting, dragging himself onto the nearest barstool. "I almost melted walking the last two blocks."

"Poor thing," Pati said dryly. "I hope your sandwich survived."

Danny held it up like a trophy. "Cubano from that corner bodega by Simonton. The one with the questionable chicken salad. And chocolate milk from Fausto's." He thudded the bottle on the bartop.

"Questionable combination," Pati chuckled.

"It's about to get even more questionable. Can you make me a Bloody Mary?"

"Gross," Pati scrunched her face in recoil at the idea of combining chocolate milk, a Cuban sandwich, and a Bloody Mary. The second two, maybe, but the chocolate milk just threw it all off. "But sure," she finally answered.

Pati began assembling the drink, but when she reached for the Tabasco, she glanced at him. "Hey—about that wine bottle at my place."

Danny blinked. "What about it?"

"Whose was it? Was it yours?"

He tilted his head. "Kind of? I mean, it was there. But I didn't open it or anything. I was drinking with a group. Some folks I met at the bonfire. There was that girl—Rachel, I think? Said she knew you."

Pati stopped stirring.

"Rachel?" she repeated.

Danny nodded, oblivious. "Yeah. Cute, kind of scrappy. Had a nose ring. Said she bartended at the Parrot with you."

Pati gave a small, stunned laugh. "Jesus Christ. Rachel is the reason I'm here right now. She was supposed to open today. Never showed. I came here after breakfast at MoonDog, figured I'd start prepping until someone else rolled in. No one did."

Danny's brow furrowed. "You think she just blew it off?"

"I don't know." Pati slid the Bloody Mary toward him. "But it's not like her."

Danny unwrapped his sandwich and took a giant bite, chewing thoughtfully. "Maybe she stayed out late. Or maybe she just crashed somewhere else. People do that all the time down here."

Pati didn't answer right away. She leaned against the bar, arms crossed, eyes distant.

"Someone was killed last night," she said finally. "On Higgs Beach. Not far from the bonfire."

Danny froze mid-chew. "Wait, what?"

"The cops came by this morning. They were questioning that weird French Canadian guy. Michel."

Danny slowly set down his sandwich. "You think it was him?"

"I think he's involved," she said. "Or knows something. But they didn't arrest him. They just… asked him to come down to the station. He didn't resist."

Danny's face darkened. "Shit. I didn't even see the cops show up. I must've blacked out."

"Yeah, well," Pati sighed. "You and half the island."

She was about to say more when her phone rang. She saw the name—John, one of the Parrot's owners—and answered quickly.

"Hey, John. I was just about to call you. I'm covering Rachel's shift, but someone's going to need to cover mine in a bit—"

"Pati," John said, cutting her off gently. "I need you to listen."

Something in his voice stopped her cold.

"There's… no easy way to say this. They found a body this morning. The one at the beach. The cops called me in because they needed someone to identify her."

Pati's stomach dropped. "Her?"

"It was Rachel."

She sat down hard on the stool behind the bar.

"No," she said, her voice barely audible. "No. That's not… she was just at the party. Danny said—he saw her—"

"I know. I know. I couldn't believe it either. I thought maybe they were wrong. But it's her. I'm on my way in now. I just needed to call you first. I know this is a lot, but I need you to hold down the fort for one more hour. Just until I get there."

Pati didn't respond. Her mouth was open but no words came out.

"I'm sorry," John added quietly. "I'll be there soon."

The line went dead.

The phone slipped from her hand and clattered softly onto the bar.

Danny stood. "Pati?"

She didn't look at him. She folded in on herself, resting her elbows on the bar, her face buried in her hands. The sob tore out of her like it had been hiding behind her ribs all day, waiting for permission to be felt.

Danny came around the bar in two quick strides, wrapping his arms around her as she broke. "Hey—hey, what's wrong? What happened?"

She couldn't get the words out at first. Just gasps and shudders and broken pieces of sentences. But eventually, through the mess of tears, she said it:

"Rachel. It was Rachel."

Danny's arms tightened. "Oh my god."

Pati shook her head, eyes squeezed shut. "She was just—she was just here. She was—"

"I know," Danny whispered. "I know."

The bar stayed empty. No new patrons walked in. And for that, Pati was grateful. She didn't have to explain. Didn't have to pretend. For just a little while longer, it was quiet again. And she could fall apart.

CHAPTER 11
BEHIND THE BAR

There was one customer at the bar when John walked in—not counting Danny, though it was debatable whether Danny qualified. He hadn't paid for a damn thing all day. Just sat there with his Cubano and his chocolate milk like the Parrot was his personal living room. Pati didn't mind, not really, but the principle of it scratched at the back of her skull.

John gave the bar a quick once-over as he entered. He looked like he hadn't slept, his graying hair sticking up in odd directions and the creases around his eyes deeper than usual. He gave a tight smile to the lone patron, nodded to Danny like he might say something, then slipped behind the bar without a word.

Pati was already reaching for a clean towel, rubbing at an invisible smear on the counter like scrubbing could ward off the wave of emotions she'd barely held back since her call with him. She didn't look up.

"You okay?" John asked softly.

Pati nodded once. "No."

John sighed and leaned both elbows on the bar,

folding his hands together. "I'm sorry you had to find out that way. I should've called sooner, but everything moved fast."

"She was supposed to be here." Pati's voice cracked despite herself. "She was supposed to be slinging drinks and bitching about her hangover and asking what shift Rob had next week."

John nodded again. "I know."

They stood in silence for a moment, the muted hum of the ceiling fan the only sound between them.

"They found her like the others," he said finally, low and grim. "Down by the water. Close to the rocks near Higgs. There was driftwood left next to her body. It had a message etched into it."

Pati's stomach turned. "What did it say?"

He looked at her with a tired kind of weight. "'By the light of the moon, it'll be alright.'"

Pati blinked, then scoffed. "What the hell does that even mean?"

John shrugged, helpless. "Some sick poetry thing, I guess."

"Did you get a picture?" she asked without thinking.

He gave her a look. "What do you think this is, a TV procedural? They don't exactly let you pull out your phone and take pictures of the crime scene."

"Right." Pati turned, grabbing a glass just so she could hold something. Her hands needed something to do. "Sorry."

John softened. "Don't apologize. I'm just—this whole thing has me upside down. She was... good. One of the good ones."

"She was my friend," Pati said, so quietly it barely registered.

They were quiet again.

Danny slid off his stool and wandered over to the bar, sandwich long gone, Bloody Mary reduced to a red smear of ice and pulp. He held the glass up expectantly.

"Another?" John asked, stepping toward the well.

Pati reached out to stop him. "No—John, this is Danny. He's not a customer. He's my brother-in-law. Kind of on an extended visit."

John paused. "Ah, okay. Got it."

Danny offered a lazy wave. "Hey."

John returned the wave with a nod. "Sorry, thought you were just a quiet drunk. Look's like you've been parked there awhile."

"Yeah, well," Danny smiled. "Haven't found a reason to leave yet."

John let out a dry chuckle, then sighed. "Listen, Pati, we've got a problem."

"We've got a lot of problems," she muttered.

"I mean with the schedule," he clarified. "Rachel was supposed to work all weekend. I don't know who we can slot in last minute."

Pati groaned and rubbed her forehead. "Don't even. I already know where this is going."

Danny leaned on the bar. "Hey, I could do it."

Both Pati and John turned to look at him.

"You bartend?" John asked, skeptical.

"Used to. Years ago. I'm a little rusty, but I can pour a drink."

Pati rolled her eyes. "Danny…"

"What?" he said, grinning. "You said you needed help. I'm here. I'm competent. Mostly."

John looked between the two of them, then back to Danny. "You got any serving violations? Fights with customers? DUI?"

Danny held up three fingers. "Nope, nope, and nope. Clean as a whistle."

"Well," John sighed. "That's better than half the people we've hired."

Pati groaned again. "So what, I have to work a double now? I'm supposed to train him for tonight's shift, too?"

"Start training him now," John said, already reaching for his phone. "I'll call Rob, see if he can relieve you in a couple hours and take over the second half. You shouldn't have to pull a double after this morning."

"Gee, thanks," Pati muttered, though the sarcasm had no teeth.

John clapped her gently on the shoulder. "I appreciate you, Pati. I really do. You've held this place down more times than I can count."

She looked at him. "Yeah, and I never thought I'd

have to do it because one of us got murdered."

His face darkened. "Me neither."

Then, he turned away and walked back toward the office in the rear, phone pressed to his ear, already mid-conversation with someone.

Danny grinned at her, clearly too pleased with himself.

"Wipe that look off your face," Pati warned, reaching below the bar for the backup bar towels. "You mess this up and I'm not covering for you."

"Noted," he said, hopping behind the bar like it was all a game.

She tossed him a towel. "First things first. You remember how to wipe down taps without flooding the place?"

Danny caught the towel one-handed. "Of course I do. I'm not an animal."

"Debatable," Pati muttered.

But a tiny smile tugged at the corner of her mouth as she showed him where everything had been moved since the last time he worked a bar. She didn't want to admit it, but having someone behind the bar with her—even him—felt a little less lonely. For now, that was enough.

Danny had barely been behind the bar ten minutes before he dropped a highball glass and knocked over the lime tray in a single, clumsy pivot.

"Jesus, Danny," Pati muttered, bending down to scoop

up scattered wedges before they rolled under the ice machine. "Are you trying to get fired before your first drink?"

"It was a test," Danny said, grinning as he grabbed a bar rag. "Wanted to see if you were paying attention."

"Oh, I'm paying attention," she said, standing up and giving him a pointed look. "And right now, you're failing."

But even as she said it, there was something almost… easy about having him there. She ran him through the current well setup, the POS system, and the new draft lines John had finally sprung for last month. Danny absorbed it all with a sort of laid-back curiosity, asking questions when he needed to but mostly nodding like things were slowly coming back to him.

"I still can't believe you guys use these plastic jiggers," he said at one point, holding one up and squinting at it like it had personally offended him. "Whatever happened to a good old-fashioned free pour?"

"Insurance premiums happened," Pati said, yanking it out of his hand and dropping it back in the speed well. "We don't eyeball it anymore. Not unless you want to be explaining to John why we're down three bottles of Tito's and have a bar full of half-conscious tourists."

"Fine, fine," he said, hands up. "Measuring it is."

To his credit, once the first few stumbles were out of the way, Danny found a rhythm. He didn't rush orders, didn't panic when the ticket printer coughed up a round of complicated cocktails, and had a surprisingly smooth banter with the few regulars who wandered in.

One of them—a sun-leathered guy named Buck who came in most days for a single light beer and a shot of well tequila—tossed Danny a wink after his second drink and said, "You're not bad, kid. You related to Pati?"

"Brother-in-law," Danny replied, sliding the shot across with a practiced flick. "She threatens to disown me daily."

"That's how you know it's real," Buck said, raising his glass. "Cheers."

Danny clinked an imaginary shot in return, then turned to Pati as Buck shuffled back to his corner stool. "You hear that? I've got fan mail already."

Pati rolled her eyes but smiled in spite of herself. "Don't let it go to your head. He calls everyone 'kid,' even the eighty-year-old regulars."

Still, she had to admit—Danny was holding his own. He remembered to card the younger-looking patrons, offered a water without being asked when someone looked too hot and too drunk, and even managed to upsell a round of call rum without sounding like a desperate cruise ship bartender.

She watched him finish a rum punch for a couple of honeymooners who'd wandered in with sunburns and matching tank tops. Danny leaned over the bar just slightly, smiled in that easy, unassuming way he had, and said, "You guys want to add a floater of dark rum on top? Brings out the pineapple and keeps the party going."

They both agreed instantly, like they'd just been offered a secret menu item. He didn't even wink afterward, Pati noticed. No cocky smirk. Just poured the floaters, handed them over, and moved on like he'd been doing this every day for years. She leaned against the back counter, watching him, arms crossed.

"Well damn," she said under her breath.

Danny turned around. "What?"

"Nothing," she said, shaking her head. "Just surprised you're not a total trainwreck."

"Thanks for the vote of confidence."

"I said not a total trainwreck."

He grinned and grabbed a new lime for garnish, slicing it with the speed of someone who'd prepped a thousand citrus wedges before. "Told you I knew what I was doing."

"Sure," she said. "And I'm Miss Congeniality."

"Pageant queen and all," he said, holding up a lime like it was a crown.

Despite everything—despite the murders, the grief clawing at the edges of her chest, the exhaustion in her bones—Pati felt something lighten. Just a little. The bar felt almost normal again for a moment.

Pati rubbed her eyes with the heel of her hand, trying to force the dull ache behind them to retreat. It was late afternoon now, though time had started to blur. The Green Parrot had picked up slightly—enough that she and Danny had been on their feet without pause for the last hour or so—but still quiet by Key West standards.

Locals mostly. A few shell-shocked tourists who either hadn't heard about the murders or were trying to drink their way past it.

She caught herself glancing toward the door, hoping each time it would swing open and Rachel would be standing there, grinning sheepishly, late as hell but alive. Every time, it was someone else.

When Rob walked in, Pati nearly dropped the bar towel she'd been nervously folding and refolding for ten minutes straight. He looked exactly like himself: tank top, salt-dried hair pulled back, sunglasses still perched on his head like he hadn't noticed he was indoors.

"I'm here," he said simply, voice low and even. "Go sit. I got it."

Pati didn't argue. She didn't have the strength. She just nodded and stepped back as Rob tossed his backpack behind the bar and gave Danny a once-over.

"This the trainee?"

"Don't scare him," Pati murmured, already easing onto a bar stool like her bones weighed twice what they should.

Danny gave a mock salute. "Name's Danny. I make Bloody Marys and break glassware."

Rob smirked. "Sounds like half the crew already."

As the two of them got to work behind the bar, Pati let herself exhale fully for the first time all day. Her body sank deeper into the cracked leather cushion. She didn't cry again—there was nothing left to come out. Just a hollow, unrelenting tiredness. Like something inside her had been carved out with a slow, dull spoon.

The door opened again and this time it was Casey and Phillip, flanked by Tia in a neon pink romper and oversized sunglasses.

"Hey!" Casey waved, beelining toward the booth. "We heard you were here. Figured we'd come by and check in. You holding up okay?"

Pati gave her a half-smile and scooted over to make room.

"Barely," she admitted. "But Rob's here now. He's training Danny, thank God. I was about to lose my mind."

"You look like you haven't slept," Phillip said gently.

"I haven't. Not really."

Tia plopped into the seat across from her, sunglasses still on. "You look like you need a damn drink."

"I look like I need a time machine," Pati said. "One that'll take me back to this morning before any of this shit started."

Tia reached across and squeezed her hand.

"I'm surprised to see you still standing," Pati added, trying to shift the conversation. "Didn't you close down the drag show last night?"

"Sure did," Tia said proudly. "I'm off for another two days. Gonna ride this wave 'til I wipe out."

Casey raised an eyebrow. "You're not worried? About the killer?"

Tia scoffed. "Not for nothing," she said, "but Black girls don't seem to be his type."

The table went quiet for a beat too long.

"I'm serious," Tia added. "All the victims? White girls. I'm not saying I'm invincible, but I'm also not worried he's lurking around corners for me."

"I don't like that you even have to think that way," Phillip muttered.

Tia shrugged. "Welcome to my life, sweetie."

Rob appeared at the booth, wiping his hands on a bar towel. "Your usual, Tia?"

"Please," she said. "And make it a double."

"So what are people saying?" Casey asked, leaning in. "Any actual info? Or just rumors?"

Pati shook her head. "Mostly rumors. But... apparently the media is already running with it. They're calling the killer 'The Frenchman.'"

"Wait—what?" Phillip sat forward. "Seriously?"

"Yeah," Pati said. "John told me. Word is, each of the women who were killed was seen talking to a man with a French accent earlier that night."

Phillip's brow furrowed. "You mean Michel."

"Allegedly," she said, voice low.

Casey tilted her head. "Has he been arrested?"

"No," Pati said. "The cops questioned him. Brought him down to the station earlier today. But I don't think they've got enough. Or maybe they're just being tight-lipped."

"So the press is ahead of the police?" Tia asked, accepting her drink from Danny. "That's comforting."

"Typical," Phillip added.

Pati leaned her elbows on the table, suddenly too tired to keep her head upright without her hands supporting it.

"It's all a mess," she said. "They're calling him 'The Frenchman' like it's some kind of noir character, but there are real people dead. Real lives ended. Rachel—" Her voice caught in her throat. "Rachel was one of them."

Casey reached out and touched her arm. "I'm so sorry."

"Me too."

The table went quiet again. The background hum of the bar filled in the gaps—bottles clinking, the low murmur of other patrons, the occasional cackle from someone playing the jukebox.

Pati stared at the water rings on the table, willing herself not to cry again. She had nothing left to say, and even less energy to fake comfort. She needed out. She needed quiet. Darkness. Blankets. Her own four walls.

"I'm gonna head out," she said, pushing back her chair.

Casey stood too. "You sure? Want company?"

"No," Pati said quickly. "Thanks, but... I need to be alone."

Danny started to say something from the bar, but Rob caught his shoulder, nodded toward Pati, and then back to the customer he was helping. Danny hesitated, then let her go.

Pati stepped out into the heavy dusk, the heat still thick even as the sun began to drop. She straddled the seat and took a deep breath.. Her limbs felt heavy, her eyes gritty, her breath too shallow. She started the moped, weaving through side streets with the familiarity of someone who could make the route half-asleep.

By the time she reached her driveway, her arms were trembling. She killed the engine and sat still for a moment, listening to the insects chirping in the still air, the distant murmur of laughter from a nearby porch. Life, somehow, still carrying on. She peeled herself off the seat, unlocked the door, and walked in without turning on the light. The cool dark swallowed her, and she dropped her keys into the bowl by the door with a metallic clink.

Her clothes hit the floor on the way to the bedroom—one item at a time, like she was shedding weight instead of fabric. The tank top. The bralette. The sweat-slicked shorts. The shoes kicked toward the wall. She climbed into bed and didn't pull the sheet up. Didn't fix the pillow. Didn't even check the time. She just let herself fall into sleep—deep, dreamless, and finally free of noise.

CHAPTER 12
LEMONADE AND LAMENT

Pati woke with her cheek stuck to the pillow and her limbs twisted in a pile of sheets that had managed to tangle themselves into a knot during the night. Her back ached. Her neck cracked when she sat up too fast. She blinked against the morning light, which was already slicing through the slats of her blinds, too bright and too insistent for the hour. She didn't check the time. She didn't need to. Her internal clock told her enough: it was already later than she'd meant to sleep.

She stretched and winced, rotating her shoulders with a grimace. There were bruises on her hips from standing behind the bar too long yesterday—no doubt pressed there by the edge of the ice well or the rubber matting. She rubbed her face, trying to scrub the residual weight of yesterday's grief off her skin.

The idea of a shower was the only thing pulling her forward. A fresh start. Or at least a cleaner one. She knew only one of those was truly possible.

She padded barefoot down the stairs, scratching at

her scalp as she went. The air in the house was stuffy with last night's heat. She was halfway to the kitchen when she saw him—Danny—sprawled across the couch again, snoring softly with one arm slung over his forehead like a Victorian ghost.

On the coffee table in front of him sat another empty bottle of red wine. Not just any red—the same bottle she'd opened for Michel the morning before, when everything had started to unravel. When Nate and Detective Morillo had come into the Parrot and quietly walked Michel out for questioning.

This bottle was drained dry. Its neck tilted slightly toward the edge of the table, a red ring blooming beneath it on the coasterless wood. Pati cursed under her breath and glanced at the throw rug, still stained from the last time Danny had crashed here and spilled something. No new damage this time, but the old splotch glared at her like a wound.

She didn't bother waking him. Just tiptoed past, grabbed her towel, and disappeared into the bathroom. The water pressure wasn't great, but it was hot, and for twenty minutes she stood beneath the stream with her eyes closed, letting the heat loosen her muscles and rinse away the film of yesterday. She shampooed her hair twice. Scrubbed her skin until it flushed pink.

Afterward, she dressed quickly—loose shorts, tank top, sneaker. Her moped sat waiting by the gate, easier, faster, and infinitely sweat-saving. But she bypassed it, unlocking her bike instead. She needed to move her body. Not mechanically, not lazily. She needed to feel her muscles work. To burn off the fog clinging to her ribs, despite the pain she was in.

The ride into Old Town from Stock Island took her past the mangroves and marinas, the shrimp boats bobbing just off the docks and the tourists crowding Duval like they didn't know—or didn't care—that people were dying here. Maybe they didn't. Maybe they thought it was just another rumor. Some weird island legend forming in real time.

The sun was brutal, already high in the sky, but the breeze off the water helped. She pedaled hard, pushing herself up the gentle inclines and coasting the downslopes with a loose grip on the handlebars. She passed the Green Parrot and its faded paint job, the familiar banyan tree stretching its arms over half the sidewalk. A cat darted across her path—one of Hemingway's six-toed sentinels, probably hunting lizards or tourists with snacks.

She kept circling. Down Angela. Up Whitehead. Around Olivia and back toward Simonton. She didn't know where she was going, only that she couldn't go home and couldn't go to the bar. Her legs moved without direction, her mind pinging like a pinball—Rachel, the driftwood, Michel, the bottle, the stain, the sadness. It all sat in her chest like damp cotton.

She dodged a pack of visitors in matching cruise ship

T-shirts, then a couple on electric scooters clearly unfamiliar with island etiquette. The woman squealed as her scooter clipped the curb. Pati didn't stop. Didn't even slow down.

She wasn't ready to see anyone. Not really. But she couldn't be alone either. That was the problem. She needed people, just not people who needed her back. By her fourth loop down Angela Street, her thighs were burning and her hands sticky on the grips. She was just about to give up and head toward the beach when a voice called out from a porch up ahead.

"If you circle this block one more time without stopping by, I'm gonna have to whoop your ass."

Pati pulled her brakes with a squeak and looked over to see Betty—Queen of the Block, unofficial mayor of Angela Street—standing on her porch in a sun-faded housedress, a smirk playing at the corners of her mouth. A half-drunk glass of lemonade sat on the small table between two wicker chairs.

Pati let out a breath she hadn't realized she'd been holding and smiled.

"You caught me," she said, turning her bike toward the porch.

"Damn right I did," Betty said. "Come on up here before I get the spray bottle."

Pati leaned her bike against the gate and climbed the steps two at a time, already feeling some of the tension in her shoulders dissolve.

"Was wondering when you'd swing by," Betty said, disappearing into the house for a moment. "Heard about what happened."

Pati sat in one of the chairs, letting the shade settle over her like a weighted blanket. The house behind her was lemon yellow, the porch painted a cool pale blue, the railings covered in hanging baskets of herbs and succulents. It smelled like basil and sunscreen and something faintly medicinal.

Betty reappeared with a second glass of lemonade and handed it over. "Drink. Then talk."

Pati took a long sip. Tart, cold, perfect. She closed her eyes for a second before opening them again.

"She was my friend," she said softly. "Rachel. She wasn't just some girl I worked with."

Betty nodded, settling into the other chair with a groan. "I know, baby. That's why I'm not making you tell the whole story unless you want to."

Pati stared into her glass. "I just… I keep thinking maybe if I hadn't gone in that day. If I hadn't been the one who found out. Or if I'd checked on her sooner."

"You're not psychic, Pati," Betty said gently. "And you're not her keeper. Don't go blaming yourself for what some monster did."

Pati nodded slowly, though the guilt still itched under her skin.

"And then there's Danny," she said after a beat. "Still passed out on my couch this morning. Drinking the same wine he opened for Michel the day the cops came."

Betty raised an eyebrow. "That boy's still here?"

"Yeah."

"You tell your sister?"

"No. Not yet. I haven't talked to Clara in a long while. Not really."

Betty's face softened, but she didn't scold. She was kind of like the Key West Fairy Godmother for all the younger folks trying to find their way. "Maybe you should. Doesn't have to be dramatic. Just a heads-up. Clean your conscience."

Pati sighed and stared out at the street. A rooster crowed somewhere in the distance.

"I'll think about it."

"Good." Betty took another sip of lemonade. "You look like you've been chased by a ghost."

"I have," Pati murmured. They sat in silence for a few minutes, just the clink of ice and the rustle of palms.

"Hey Betty," Pati broke the silence. "Random question, but does Casey still live in your bungalow? Or did she move out into Phillip's place?"

"Oh those love birds had to live together," Betty laughed. "Why? You looking for a place closer to work?"

Pati smiled. "Nah, but I was just thinking about them. They're good people. They're what my sister doesn't understand about this place: the really amazing people you can find."

Betty nodded and smiled in approval. Pati stood and thanked Betty, promising to check in again soon. She grabbed her bike and took off down Angela Street, her next stop unclear, her thoughts heavy, but her chest—just slightly—less tight.

Pati coasted her bike up toward the bench near the big banyan tree on White Street. It was one of her favorite places to think—shaded, quiet, and tucked away just enough from the foot traffic to feel like a secret. The tree's roots spilled over the sidewalk like ancient fingers, curling into the dirt, massive and gnarled. Pati leaned her bike gently against one of them and plopped down on the bench, still slightly damp from the humid morning air.

She pulled out her phone and stared at the cracked screen, the soft hiss of cicadas in her ears. For a long moment, she just scrolled—mindless, mechanical—through photos, text chains, anything to distract herself from the decision at hand. The phone felt heavier than it should've.

On one hand, she needed to call Clara. She wasn't even sure if it was a moral obligation or just the weight of guilt pressing on her chest. Danny was her sister's husband, after all—soon-to-be ex or not—and he was now sleeping on her couch like some rum-soaked stray. It wasn't romantic. It wasn't even really complicated. But it felt... sticky. Like something that needed cleaning up.

On the other hand, she needed to know who killed Rachel.

She stared down at her contact list, thumb hovering somewhere between "Clara" and "Nate R. – FantasyFest Cop." She didn't want to talk to Clara. She didn't want the sighs or the passive-aggressive commentary or the silence on the other end of the line. She wanted answers. She wanted justice. Hell, she'd settle for a direction.

Her thumb moved. Texted: *Any updates? Hanging at the big banyan tree if you're free.*

The reply came faster than she expected.

Nate: *I'm actually not far from you. Give me five?*

She didn't reply. Just locked her phone and sank a little further into the bench, elbows resting on her knees. The breeze stirred a few fallen leaves across the pavement, and Pati followed their slow, lazy shuffle with her eyes until she saw a shadow stretch over the sidewalk.

Nate was in plainclothes, which made him look more like a grad student than a cop—tall, slightly hunched, hair rumpled from the humidity. He wore a T-shirt with some faded band logo she couldn't place and a pair of board shorts that looked like they hadn't been washed in days. But the badge clipped to his belt was unmistakable.

"Hey," he said, lowering himself to sit beside her.

Pati didn't waste time. "What's the news?"

He exhaled, slow. "We had to release Michel Moreau."

"What?" Pati blinked at him. "Why?"

"DNA doesn't match."

She frowned. "You have DNA?"

He gave her a look. "You didn't hear that from me."

"No, of course not," she said, waving a hand. "Let me guess. You pulled it off the driftwood?"

That gave Nate pause. "How do you know about the driftwood?"

Pati tilted her head. "Rumor mill's still good for something."

He chuckled, but there was no humor in it. "Well, yeah. We got a partial profile. Enough to know it wasn't Moreau."

"So what now?"

"We're still following up on sightings. The last two victims were both seen with a man matching a certain description—white guy, about five-ten, French accent. But it's all loose. Every witness had alcohol in their system. Some don't even agree on the hair color."

Pati blew out a breath. "But you're still calling him a suspect?"

"He's no longer a suspect," Nate said firmly. "He was in custody overnight. We had nothing to hold him on. And now…"

"Speak of the devil," he added, his tone shifting. He nodded behind her.

Pati turned.

Michel walked toward them with long, furious strides. He looked disheveled, but not in the rumpled, sleep-deprived way Nate did. Michel looked purposefully undone—shirt wrinkled, sandals half buckled, his linen pants streaked with salt spray like he'd taken a rage-walk down the seawall and back again.

"Vous m'avez insulté devant tout le monde!" he snapped, launching into a tirade in rapid-fire French that Pati barely caught half of. She stood, startled, but he was already gesturing sharply in her direction. "C'est impardonnable! Une accusation si vile, si—"

"Michel," Nate cut in, stepping forward.

Michel spun toward him. "You. At least you had the decency to ask questions before assuming I was some kind of killer."

Nate raised a calming hand. "Dr. Moreau, it's good to see you under different circumstances."

"Doctor?" Pati repeated, blinking.

Michel turned back to her with a look of absolute offense. "Yes. Doctor. I am a professor of French literature and Francophone studies. Université de Montréal."

He straightened his spine like that should've explained everything.

"I specialize in early to mid-20th-century French culture—specifically literature, performance, and the postwar cultural ethos. I'm here on sabbatical. Or was."

Pati gaped. "And this is relevant how?"

Michel scowled. "Because everything about me—the accent, the jukebox, my interest in Piaf—it all suddenly made me some kind of... suspect. An object of fear and suspicion."

"You have to admit," Pati said, arms crossed, "you were acting pretty sketchy."

His eyebrows shot up. "Sketchy?"

"You were skulking around the bar like a noir villain. Always at the jukebox. Talking to women and then disappearing the moment someone looked your way. And then when the cops came to get you, you went silent. No protest. Just walked out like you'd already planned it."

Michel grimaced. "Because I knew better than to make a scene. I assumed the truth would sort itself out."

"And I assumed the guy matching the killer's profile hanging out at my bar might be worth keeping an eye on," she snapped.

They stared at each other for a moment, the banyan tree casting its tangled shadow over both of them. Then Pati shook her head, as if trying to rattle something loose.

"You know what really got me?" she said, her voice lower now, quieter. "That day—before Rachel died—you were at the jukebox. Played 'La Vie en Rose' like three times in a row. I made some crack, said you must really love that song. You looked at me like I'd just insulted your mother."

"I don't love it. I respect it. People think it's a love song but really it's a lament. Because Piaf lost the love of her life in a crash, and the song's not about romance, it's about grief. Anyone who hears it as a love song isn't really listening. They're 'dreaming.' Just idiots clinging to pretty delusions. The entire post-war chanson tradition—Piaf, Trenet, Montand—was shaped by mourning, not romance. It was a cultural reckoning. 'La Vie en Rose' is not a celebration. It's a mask. A way to survive."

Pati and Nate blinked blankly at Dr. Moreau.

"Oh forget it!" he said, throwing his hands up. "I'll be going to the mainland now," he said over his shoulder as he walked away. "Palm Beach. Then home. I've had quite enough of Key West."

"I can't imagine why," Pati muttered.

"I hope you all enjoy your paranoia," he called back. "I'll enjoy my country's healthcare system and the dignity of not being interrogated by amateurs."

And with that, he stalked away, his long legs carrying him toward the corner where the banyan's roots gave way to asphalt.

Pati sank back onto the bench.

Nate chuckled. "Whew. He is steamed."

She groaned. "That man is a pretentious wreck."

"French-toasted," Nate said with a grin.

Pati glared at him.

"What?" he shrugged. "Gallows humor."

Her head fell into her hands. "I feel like shit."

"Why?"

"I don't know. Maybe because I accused a completely innocent man of being a serial killer? And now Rachel's still dead and we're back to square one."

Nate didn't speak right away. He sat down beside her again, this time a little closer. "Look, I can't tell you everything. But what I can say is—we're not back to square one. We're building a profile. We've got patterns now. And we're getting more resources. The higher-ups finally believe it's the same guy."

Pati looked at him. "So what now?"

"Now we chase ghosts," he said, standing. His phone buzzed, and he checked it with a quick glance. "And I chase calls."

He sighed, looking apologetic. "I've gotta run. But hey—don't beat yourself up. You were looking out for your people."

"I was wrong."

"Sometimes being wrong is how we get closer to right."

She nodded slowly. "Be safe."

"You too."

He jogged off, phone pressed to his ear.

Pati leaned back against the bench, exhaling slowly, eyes fixed on the twisted sky of branches above her.

For the first time in days, she didn't know what to do next. But she knew she couldn't go back to pretending. Not now.

Not when the killer was still out there.

And Rachel's voice, once loud and unmistakable, was now gone for good.

CHAPTER 13
ONE MORE FOR THE LIST

Schooner Wharf was buzzing. The smell of beer and brine clung to the air, mingling with sweat and the occasional waft of fried conch drifting in from the kitchen. A rusted fan spun lazily above the bar, doing more for the illusion of relief than actual airflow.

Pati swung her leg over the stool closest to the tap handles, her elbows resting on the sun-sticky wood. She'd barely settled when Rory materialized from behind the bar, sliding a tall, sweating pint in front of her.

"Try this," they said, leaning in with a grin. "It's new. From that microbrewery up in Big Pine. Mango-something. They call it Island Mirage, which sounds like a cologne from a gas station, but it's not terrible."

Pati raised the glass and sniffed. "You trying to get me drunk on fruit salad?"

"I'd never," Rory said, mock-offended. "I'm just expanding your palate."

They flashed her a smile that crinkled the edges of their salt-kissed face. Rory's tan was deeper than usual, the sun carving new creases around their eyes. Their hair was pulled back today, salt-and-pepper strands haloed by a bandana that looked like it had been bleached by both ocean spray and tequila regret. They weren't much older than Pati—maybe three or four years, tops—but the sun had aged them in that quintessential Keys way: kissed, slapped, and kissed again.

Pati took a sip. Not bad. Bright, a little sweet, but with a citrusy bitterness that lingered in a way she didn't mind. "Alright," she said. "I'll allow it."

Rory winked. "High praise."

For a while, they didn't talk. Just let the bar noise fill the spaces between them. Tourists laughed too loud behind them, a guy with a guitar strummed something vaguely Buffett-adjacent near the back patio, and a dog barked in the distance like it had opinions.

Then Rory leaned in again, voice lower now. "So?"

Pati raised a brow. "So what?"

"You gonna tell me what's eating at you or just sit there pretending you like that beer more than you do?"

Pati sighed and stared at the condensation slipping down the glass. "It's all this murder stuff. It's been haunting my bar, my shifts, my fucking dreams. I thought I knew who it was."

Rory's gaze sharpened. "That weird song guy that was hangin' around the Parrot?"

Pati nodded, knowing how fast word of "someone to watch" on the island spread between bartenders. "I really thought it was him. The way he moved, the things he said, the jukebox, the fucking song…"

"La Vie en Creepy," Rory muttered.

Pati huffed out a laugh. "Exactly. And Rachel—" Her voice caught. She swallowed. "Rachel thought so too. She got the creeps off him. And now… she's gone."

The weight of it dropped between them like a cinder block.

"I'm sorry," Rory said, serious now. "Rachel was a good one. Sharp as hell. You don't get many like her."

Pati nodded. Her fingers toyed with the corner of a coaster. "And the thing is, Michel's been cleared. DNA or whatever. They ruled him out."

Rory didn't speak for a moment. Then, "That doesn't make him less weird."

"No," Pati agreed. "But it means someone else did this. Is still doing this."

Rory leaned back, folded their arms. "You think it's a local?"

"I don't know. Could be someone moving up or down the chain. But it's like… he's always one step ahead. Always just far enough away to disappear again. And now that Michel's off the table—" She cut off, frustrated. "I don't know where to point my fear anymore."

Before Rory could respond, a man at the far end of the bar leaned over, his sunburnt neck glistening with sweat. "Sorry to interrupt," he said, voice gravelly with salt and cigarettes. "Did you say something about those murders?"

Pati blinked. "Yeah. Why?"

He shook his head, wiping sweat from his forehead with a napkin. "Just came from Fort Zach. Cops are all over it. Another body."

Everything stilled.

"What?" Rory said.

"Another girl," the man said. "Near the rocks by the shore. Tape's up, people being pushed back. I only caught a glimpse before they moved us along."

Pati's stomach clenched. "You're sure?"

"Dead sure," the man said grimly. "That makes five, right? Islamorada, Marathon, Stock Island, Higgs Beach, and now Fort Zachary."

Rory let out a low whistle. "Jesus."

Pati was already reaching for her phone. Her fingers moved before her mind did, texting Nate: Are you at Fort Zachary right now?

A moment passed. Then three dots. Then: How do you know that?

She didn't answer. Instead, she tossed a few bills on the bar, drained the last of her beer, and stood.

"That new brew?" she said to Rory, voice flat. "Not bad. But not to die for."

Rory grimaced. "Really?"

She shrugged. "Poor choice of words."

"Yeah, well," Rory said, eyes narrowing, "you be careful, Pati."

"I always am," she lied, already moving.

Her bike leaned where she'd left it against the patio

railing. She kicked off and started pedaling hard, the breeze not enough to cool her.

Five girls.

Five bodies.

Someone had to be stopped.

And it wasn't going to happen by waiting around for another one to show up in the sand.

By the time Pati rolled up to Fort Zachary Taylor, the sun had melted past the horizon, leaving the sky bruised and moody. A few lingering streaks of orange clung stubbornly to the west, but the rest of the world was already slipping into indigo. The road to the beach was blocked—an unmarked cruiser parked sideways near the main path, headlights dimmed but engine still humming.

She slowed her bike and dismounted, walking it closer until she spotted the tape. Yellow and fluttering in the evening breeze, it cordoned off the area in that jarring, unmistakable way—like caution itself had grown legs and planted flags in the sand.

There were only a handful of people left milling about. A couple of uniformed officers stood near the treeline, one speaking into a radio, the other shining a flashlight into the scrubby undergrowth. The crowd had already been pushed back. No gawkers remained. Just the low thrum of insects, the distant lap of waves, and the heavy silence that followed tragedy.

Pati saw him near the edge of the beach, standing just inside the tape line. Nate.

He wore jeans and a faded green button down, sleeves pushed up to his elbows, a clipboard tucked under one arm. His expression was locked in that grim cop-mask—neutral, unreadable, a little too practiced. He saw her as she approached and stepped forward immediately.

"Pati," he said, his voice low but firm. "You shouldn't be here."

"I heard," she said, her bike squeaking as she guided it up the sandy path. "Someone at Schooner's told me. Is it true?"

He didn't answer right away. Just looked at her, like he was weighing how much to say.

She let the silence hang. Let him see it in her face—that she wasn't going to leave without something. Finally, Nate sighed and stepped a little closer, out of earshot of the other officers.

"There's a piece of driftwood," he said, his voice barely above a whisper. "Same handwriting. Same placement."

Pati's blood ran cold.

"What did it say?"

He looked past her, toward the surf. The moon was rising now, silver and distant, just cresting the palm line.

"'By the light of the moon, it'll be all right,'" Nate said. "Same as Rachel's."

She didn't speak for a moment. Her mouth had gone dry.

"Do you have an ID yet?" she asked.

"Not yet," Nate said. "No wallet. No phone. Same MO—hair brushed, hands folded. Like she was tucked in to say her prayers."

Pati let go of her bike and crossed her arms over her chest. The wind off the water chilled the sweat that clung to the back of her neck.

"Whoever it is," Nate added, "we'll know soon. We're pulling prints. But... it's not looking good."

Pati's jaw tightened. "You mean, you think it's someone local?"

"I mean," Nate said gently, "there are only so many girls that fit the profile left on this island."

"Really?" Pati said, incredulously. "Not a lot of girls with longish brown hair and blue eyes?"

"Well, they also have to be in their 20s or 30s, judging by the pattern."

"Seriously, Nate? And you still don't have any leads?"

"We had a lead," he said. "Michel. Turned out he was just a creep with a broken heart and a nostalgia complex he turned into a career in academia."

She didn't want to admit how much that rattled her. How much she'd needed it to be Michel. Because if it wasn't him, then it was still out there. And getting closer.

"I want to help," she said.

Nate's brow furrowed. "Pati..."

"I'm serious," she pushed. "You know I've been around all of this from the beginning. I've talked to Michel more than anyone. I knew Rachel. I know this island. I know what's normal and what's not."

"I know," he said. "But this is a crime scene. I can't let you in. Not even close."

"Goddammit, Nate—" Her voice cracked. "I can't just sit around while this keeps happening. I'm not built for that."

"I know you're not," he said, stepping between her and the tape. "But I'm telling you, if I let you through, and something gets compromised, even by accident, I lose my badge and the families lose their answers. I can't risk that."

Her fists clenched at her sides. "So what am I supposed to do? Just wait around to find out if this killer takes another person I care about? While he terrifies everyone on the chain?"

"I'm telling you to be careful," he said. "Watch who's around you. Watch who shows up where they shouldn't. I know you want to catch this guy, but if you start playing vigilante—"

"I'm not," she snapped. "But I also can't pretend this isn't happening all around me."

"I'm not asking you to," he said. "Just don't get yourself killed trying to prove something."

They stood like that for a long moment—two figures in the moonlight, the tape fluttering between them.

Finally, Pati exhaled. "You'll call me if you learn more?"

Nate nodded. "If I can."

She reached down and picked her bike back up. Her fingers trembled slightly, but she didn't let it show.

As she turned to go, she muttered, "By the light of the moon, it'll be all right…"

Nate glanced at her. "What?"

She shook her head. "It just sounds like something someone would write in a journal. A wish. Not a threat."

"Maybe it's both," he said.

She didn't take the main road back. Instead, Pati veered left out of the park entrance and cut toward the shoreline. Her tires crunched over crushed coral and soft dirt, the path lit only by the moon. The wind had picked up slightly, tugging at her tank top and whistling through the palms.

She didn't want to go straight home. Not yet. Not with that phrase still echoing in her skull. Not with the image of Rachel's folded hands burned into the backs of her eyes.

She needed space. Air. Time.

She pedaled past the cemetery, its white tombs glowing faintly in the moonlight. Past the marina where the sailboats bobbed gently like sleeping whales. Past a group of kids lighting sparklers in a driveway, their laughter trailing after her like ghosts.

She turned down Whitehead, then again toward Catherine Street, letting the route stretch, letting the silence settle. By the time she got home, her legs were sore and her throat was dry. The porch light was still on, casting a soft glow over the cracked steps.

She leaned her bike against the railing and climbed the steps to her door. She was home. She was safe. And it looked like Danny was inside, so she wouldn't be alone. As she opened the door, she smelled her citrus candle— Danny must've lit it. And then she heard it. The sound of a scratchy gramophone cut her to the bone— "La Vie en Rose" arpeggios.

CHAPTER 14
A SONG I'VE HEARD BEFORE

Pati almost couldn't believe her ears. It wasn't the modern, crystal-clear version. Not even the dusty jukebox cut that Michel had played that day at the Green Parrot. This was something else entirely—so old it sounded haunted. The static hissed in waves behind Édith Piaf's voice, her vibrato warbling through the speaker like it had been exhumed from another century.

Pati stepped further inside, quietly, unsure if she wanted to interrupt whatever strange ritual was unfolding. And there was Danny. In the middle of the living room, barefoot, his shirt hanging loose over wrinkled shorts, dancing alone. Arms curved gently in the air as if he were holding someone. Chin tilted downward. Eyes closed.

He didn't see her at first. He was somewhere else entirely. Somewhere far from Stock Island. Her voice caught before it reached her throat. She watched for another moment, frozen.

The speaker perched on the counter blinked faintly,

its soft blue light flickering with the music's pulse.

"Danny?"

He startled, his body stiffening mid-step. His eyes snapped open, and when they landed on her, something in his expression broke apart.

"Shit," he breathed. "Pati. I didn't hear you come in."

She didn't move. "What… are you doing?"

Danny gave a laugh that collapsed under its own weight. "Honestly? I don't know. Just… got lost in it."

The music still played behind them—now the final stretch of the track, Piaf's voice dropping into that fragile, aching tone that made you feel like you were eavesdropping on something intimate.

Danny crossed to the speaker and paused it. The silence that followed wasn't peaceful. It rang in the space like a warning.

"I thought you hated that song," Pati said carefully. "You told me Clara picked it. That it never meant anything to you."

"I didn't hate it," he said. "I just didn't understand it."

She gave him a look. "And now you do?"

He sank into the armchair, the tension leaving his shoulders in visible waves. "No. But I'm trying to."

Pati dropped her bag beside the couch and lowered herself to the edge of the cushion, elbows on her knees. "Danny, what's going on?"

He rubbed his palms over his face, like he was trying to wipe himself out of existence.

After a long pause, he stood and dug his wallet out of his back pocket.

"What is it?" Pati asked.

He opened it slowly and handed her a small polaroid photo. Faded and soft at the edges. Clara and Danny. College. Probably late sophomore year, judging by the scuffed messenger bag Danny wore and the big hoop earrings Clara had gone through a phase with. They were standing in front of a campus fountain, Danny's arm draped over Clara's shoulders like it belonged there, her laugh mid-spill across the photo's grain.

Pati smiled despite herself. "God. This was forever ago."

Danny's voice was hoarse. "I've had that photo in my wallet for a decade. It's falling apart, but I can't bring my-self to take it out."

He sat again, but not in the armchair. This time, on the floor, legs stretched out, the photo still clutched in one hand.

"I came here," he said, "because I didn't know where else to go. Clara and I haven't spoken since May. She took me off the phone plan. She stopped replying to emails. Just… radio silence."

Pati leaned back against the couch. "I figured she needed space."

"So did I," he said. "But then I started dreaming about her. Every night. Not even about the fights. Just… regular things. Laughing in the kitchen. Watching bad movies. Sitting in traffic and singing along to The Cranberries.

And I kept thinking, what if we could get back to that? Before everything soured?"

He swallowed.

"Our honeymoon was in Paris," he added, voice quieter now. "We stayed in this tiny apartment in the Marais. Walked the streets with no plans. We had red wine every night, cheap stuff from the corner store. And we danced to this old Bluetooth speaker one night on Bastille Day—right in the middle of the apartment, barefoot, drunk, stupidly in love."

He looked up at her, tears in his eyes. "That's why I've been drinking so much red wine. That's why that song is stuck in my head. I'm not trying to be creepy. I'm just… I miss her. I miss who we were."

Pati felt her defenses cracking. Not shattering—but shifting. She'd known Danny a long time. Long enough to recognize his drama from his devastation. This wasn't the performance of a heartbroken man. It was the collapse of one.

"I know I'm pathetic," he said.

"You're not."

"I showed up here thinking maybe if I could breathe the same air I did back then—get close to the salt and the heat and the music and everything Clara always hated—I could find the parts of myself I liked."

He exhaled, wiping at his face with the hem of his shirt.

"Maybe I thought if I danced in the living room to the same song we danced to in Paris, it would mean something. That she'd feel it. That somehow… she'd remember what it was like to love me."

Pati's voice was soft. "Danny…"

"I know it's stupid."

"It's not stupid," she said. "It's sad. But it's not stupid."

Danny leaned his head back against the ottoman, looking up at the ceiling as if the answer to everything might be written there.

"I keep wondering," he said, "what I would say to her if I had one more night. Just one. No fighting. No bills. No passive-aggressive digs. Just wine. Music. That damn song."

Pati thought of the driftwood. Of the bodies. Of the moon. Of Michel. She didn't want to think of Michel now.

"I wish I could go back," he whispered. "Back to that apartment. Back to the feeling of the rain on the windows and her body against mine. We were stupid in love. And I'd give anything to be that stupid again."

Silence stretched between them like tidewater—warm, full of pull.

Pati leaned forward and reached out, placing her hand over his.

"You still could call her," she said. "Maybe she won't pick up. But maybe she will. Maybe you just need to say the things you've been dancing around."

Danny gave a watery smile. "What if I don't know how to anymore?"

Pati squeezed his hand. "Start with the truth."

Danny hadn't moved from the floor. The old photo lay between them like an offering, edges curled inward with time and too much handling. Pati sat cross-legged on the couch now, the drink she had poured still untouched on the table beside her.

"You know," she said softly, "Clara and I were never really close. Not like sisters are supposed to be."

Danny looked up.

"We played the part when we had to—holidays, school pictures, family cookouts—but we were opposites. Total opposites. Even as kids."

She rested her chin in her palm and let herself slip backward in time.

"Clara was always… right. Like, capital-R right. Straight As, color-coded binders, teacher's pet but somehow not annoying about it. She wore bows in her hair until high school and never once got a grass stain on her uniform skirt. Meanwhile, I was the one with bruised knees and a baseball cap I refused to take off."

Danny smiled faintly. "I can picture that."

"She used to call me 'gremlin' when we were little," Pati continued. "I think she meant it with affection. Mostly. I'd come inside covered in dirt or paint or some combination of the two, and she'd wrinkle her nose and say, 'Mom, the gremlin's loose again.' I'd take it as a compliment."

"She was always… polished," Danny said. "I guess that's what drew me to her at first. She just had this way of knowing where she was going."

Pati snorted. "She always had a plan. A backup plan. And then a spreadsheet for if both plans failed."

Danny laughed, but it faded fast.

"She hated how chaotic I was," Pati added. "Even when we were teenagers, she'd say stuff like, 'You'd be prettier if you just tried a little,' or 'Not everything has to be a performance, Pati.' She didn't get that for me, chaos was the only way I knew how to feel… free."

She reached for her glass, turning it slowly in her hand. "But I always envied her, in a way. People trusted her. Listened to her. She never had to yell to be heard."

Danny's expression softened. "She always said you were brave."

Pati blinked. "She said that?"

He nodded. "We had a fight once. Years ago. I don't even remember what it was about. Something stupid— credit card statements, maybe. But I remember yelling something like, 'God, why can't you just let go for once?' And she got real quiet and said, 'Not everyone gets to be like my sister. Pati just… leaps. She's not afraid to screw up. She's not afraid of being wrong.'"

Pati looked away, eyes burning unexpectedly. "She never told me that."

"She probably didn't know how," Danny said gently. "She's not great with… softness."

"No," Pati agreed. "She's good at building walls and calling it structure."

Danny exhaled. "I thought if I could break through that structure… I'd get to her heart again."

Pati smiled sadly. "You probably did once. But you also became part of the structure. And when it cracked, she didn't know what to do with it."

Silence settled for a moment. The hum of the fridge kicked in. A distant car passed, its headlights tracing a brief silver arc across the window.

"I think I made peace with her being distant," Pati said. "It's easier than hoping she'll be someone she's not. But it doesn't mean I don't miss her sometimes."

Danny nodded, running a hand through his hair. "Same."

"She hated the Keys," Pati added. "Too humid. Too loud. Too many chickens."

Danny grinned. "And you loved all of that."

"Still do," she said. "The mess, the heat, the weirdos—it's home. I think it scared her, how comfortable I was in the chaos."

"She always said she was proud of you," Danny offered. "Even if she didn't always get it. She respected that you chose your own life."

Pati leaned back and exhaled, the tension slowly draining from her shoulders.

"I just wish she said it out loud," she murmured.

Danny reached for the photo again, admiring it.

"Maybe you two will talk again," he said. "When things settle."

Pati looked at him, a little smile ghosting the corner of her mouth.

"If the world ever settles," she said. "I'll think about it."

Danny had gone quiet. His earlier tears still clung to the soft skin under his eyes, but his shoulders had stiffened. He was holding something back now, that much was clear.

Pati felt it before he said anything. That shift in the room, like the air had thickened.

"Pati," he said quietly, not meeting her eyes, "I need to tell you something."

She tilted her head, bracing herself. "Okay…"

"I wasn't in Nashville when I called you," he said. "I hadn't just bought a plane ticket that morning."

Pati frowned. "What?"

"I'd been here. In the Keys. For a week. Before I called."

Her stomach dropped. "What do you mean you were already here?"

"I didn't know how to say it. I didn't want you to think I was some... stalker or something. Or that I was unhinged."

"Well," she said sharply, sitting up straighter, "lying to me definitely helped with that."

"I didn't lie—"

"You absolutely lied."

Danny winced. "Okay. I lied. But I didn't mean to. I mean, I wasn't planning it. I just… I came down after Clara kicked me out. I was a mess. Couldn't sleep. Couldn't think. So I drove. I didn't even pack properly. I just got in the car and ended up here."

"In the Keys," Pati repeated. "The last place you were happy."

He nodded.

Pati stood and started pacing. "You told me you bought a bike from two kids, biked from the airport, went to my place, then came to the bar—all in the same day. But that was a story."

"I thought it'd be easier if you believed it was impulsive," he said. "If you thought I hadn't had time to unravel. But the truth is… I unraveled before I even got here. I've been losing my mind for months. This was the only place that made any sense."

"So instead of calling," she snapped, "you just skulked around town for a week and waited until it was convenient?"

"No!" he said, rising to his feet. "I just didn't want to bring my mess to your door. I wanted to figure out if I was even capable of asking for help without wrecking everything."

"You did wreck everything," she shot back. "You could've told me. I opened my home to you, Danny. I let you into my life when you were at rock bottom, and you've been keeping secrets the whole time."

"I didn't mean to hurt you," he said softly.

"But you did."

Her chest burned. Not just from the lie, but from the betrayal of trust. She had let her guard down—for him. She had begun to believe his sincerity. But now, all of it felt suspect.

"What else are you lying about?" she asked, voice low.

Danny's eyes widened. "Nothing."

"How can I believe that?"

Silence.

She shook her head and turned toward the hallway. "I'm going to bed."

"Pati—"

"No," she said, not looking back. "I need space. Real space. Sleep on the couch. I don't care. Just don't knock on my door."

She disappeared into her bedroom, leaving Danny alone with his tattered photo, tear-streaked face, and half-drunk bottle of wine.

The ceiling fan spun in lazy, wobbly arcs, but it did nothing for the heat building in Pati's chest. She lay on her back, eyes wide open, the moonlight slicing through the blinds and striping her ceiling in silver.

The house was quiet now. Too quiet. Even the cicadas outside had gone still, like they sensed something brewing. She kept hearing the crackle of that damn song in her mind, distorted and dusty. Clara's wedding song. Her "perfect day." Pati had always rolled her eyes at Clara's decision to have a string quartet and a French vocalist perform a decades-old chanson during the first dance. "Pretentious," she'd muttered to Rachel under her breath, sipping cheap champagne and trying not to fidget in the itchy satin bridesmaid dress.

But now, lying there with the weight of everything pressing on her chest, she remembered something creepy ol' Dr. Michel Moreau had said: "It's not a love song; it's a lament. Piaf sings it like a woman who's desperate to believe love still exists."

At the time, she'd rolled her eyes at what a loon he was, even if he was innocent of murder. Now she wasn't so sure what to make of it. Maybe Clara and Danny had been doomed from the first dance. Words had power. Songs had weight. And Clara had chosen that song to begin her marriage. A song full of longing and hope wrapped around an ache. Pati should've seen it then. The cracks under the perfect surface.

Her mind drifted.

Back to the driftwood.

Back to the words etched in careful strokes: By the light of the moon, it'll be all right.

What did it mean? A message? A signature? A threat?

She stared at the ceiling, throat tight. She couldn't protect everyone. But she could try. And she would.

CHAPTER 15
AN ANGEL'S TAUNT

The dream began the way all the worst ones did—quietly. Pati walked alone on the beach, barefoot, the sand cool and fine between her toes. The moon hung fat and low above the water, silvering the waves in slow pulses. Everything was soft. Too soft. Like the air had been wrapped in cotton and every sound had to fight to be heard. Music drifted toward her—not from a single place, but everywhere at once. Faint and flickering, like it came on the tide. A violin, maybe. Or an old record playing on a cracked speaker just beyond the dunes. "La Vie en Rose."

Of course.

She walked slowly, the hem of her sleep-shirt brushing her knees, her arms bare to the breeze. Her bike was gone. Her shoes too. She didn't remember coming here. But she knew where she was.

Fort Zachary. But wrong. Off. As though someone had rebuilt it from memory and left out a few details. The trees along the edge of the sand were too tall. The horizon line was warped. The sand glittered faintly, unnaturally, as if dusted in glass.

She moved forward anyway. The music swelled, then dipped. Swelled, then dipped. Like breathing. Or like the tide. Her eyes scanned the beach, looking for something she didn't want to find. And then she saw it.

A piece of driftwood nestled in the sand ahead, just at the edge of the waterline. It jutted out at an angle, half-buried, the kind of thing you'd miss if you weren't already looking for it.

Pati crouched and reached for it. The moment her fingers touched the wood, the music stopped. Dead silence.

She turned the driftwood over. Etched into it—those same words. Again. By the light of the moon, it'll be all right. She blinked. And then the beach was full of shadows. Dozens of them.

They weren't there a moment ago, but now they were all around her—shapes emerging from the darkness like figures from a stage fog. Pati stumbled back, the driftwood still in her hand, her breath catching in her throat. The figures moved slowly, like sleepwalkers. As they stepped into the moonlight, she saw the truth of them. Bodies. No longer shadows moving, but still, cold bodies. Laid out carefully, each one placed like a ritual offering. Hands bound in front of them in a posture of prayer. Hair spread behind their heads like a dark halo. All young. All with brown hair. All with blue-tinted skin.

Pati's lungs seized. Some of the faces she didn't recognize. But others—that girl with the dolphin tattoo—she'd ordered a piña colada and tipped big. The one from Stock

Island. Kayla? Kelsey? Her face had been on a flyer, stapled to a telephone pole by the marina. The sweet-looking girl who'd come into the Parrot last month with a notebook and a sunburn. And then—Rachel.

Right there, closest to her. Her eyes were closed now. Her lips slack. Her hands bound in that same tight knot of nylon rope. Her hair fanned around her, catching the moonlight and glowing like copper.

Pati dropped the driftwood.

"No," she whispered. "No no no—"

She took a step back.

Then another.

The tide rolled in behind her.

And with it came the sound.

A hum.

Low and bone-deep, like it rose from the ocean floor itself. It vibrated through her ribs. The same hum she'd felt at Higgs Beach, during the bonfire. The same one she'd tried to ignore.

It grew louder.

The sand shifted.

The girls began to breathe.

Not alive, not quite—but moving.

Hands twitching.

Eyes fluttering.

Rachel's fingers curled inward.

"No—" Pati whispered again. She turned to run, but the beach stretched forever now, an impossible plane of glowing sand and moon-painted water. The horizon had vanished. The music came back—twisted, reversed, playing "La Vie en Rose" backward.

A voice echoed behind her. Soft. Familiar.

"You can't save them."

She turned. No one.

"You were always just watching."

The driftwood burned in the sand, smoking as though it had caught fire from nothing at all.

"You can't protect anyone, Pati."

The bodies sat up. Their mouths opened. And the hum screamed.

Pati woke up with a sharp gasp, sitting bolt upright in bed. Her sheets were damp. Her chest heaved. Her heart pounded so hard it felt like it might snap her ribs apart. She reached instinctively for her phone. 6:03 a.m. An hour before her alarm.

The room was dim, shadows stretching long across the floor. Outside, the first hints of morning had begun to lighten the blinds, moonlight replaced by a faint pink haze.

She pressed her palms to her eyes and tried to slow her breathing. Just a dream. She repeated it like a mantra, but the weight in her chest remained. She swung her legs out of bed and sat there for a long time, elbows on her knees, staring at the floor.

That phrase—By the light of the moon, it'll be all right. She heard it again in her mind, not as a whisper now but as a chant. A promise. A threat.

But what did it mean? What kind of person carved those words into driftwood and laid it at the feet or in the hands of murdered girls? She wrapped her arms around herself.

The image of Rachel lying there, moonlight in her hair, rope tight around her wrists—it was too much. Pati wanted to scream. To kick something. But all she could do was sit in the silence and shake.

She thought again of the wedding. Of that damn song. Of Clara—perfect Clara—who had chosen it as her first dance without irony, as though "La Vie en Rose" were some romantic ideal and not what it really was: a fantasy built on grief. A desperate attempt to believe. I see life through rose-colored glasses. That was the lie, wasn't it? And what if whoever was doing this—whoever kept placing those words like breadcrumbs—was trying to tell the same lie?

That everything was okay. That things could be made right again. That the moonlight could fix what the world broke.

Pati stood, legs unsteady, and crossed to the window. Outside, the moon was just beginning to dip. The sea breeze rustled the hibiscus leaves near the porch. Danny's bike leaned crooked against the railing. She pressed her forehead to the glass and watched her breath build condensation on the window.

Pati didn't even bother to check if Danny was awake. She could still hear his soft, congested snores coming from the living room, muffled by the couch cushions. A trail of socks, a crumpled hoodie, and a balled-up paper napkin littered the floor like some kind of toddler had tornadoed through. She clenched her jaw, grabbed her keys, and slipped out the door.

The sky was just beginning to brighten, that soft pre-dawn hue that made everything feel a little muted, like the island was still waking up. She wheeled her moped out from under the overhang and didn't bother with her helmet. The wind would feel good on her face. The engine sputtered, then caught with a low rumble that felt almost too loud for the hour.

She rode slowly, taking roads through sleepy neighborhoods where palms cast long shadows and the smell of dew-soaked hibiscus clung to the air. A few porch lights flickered on. Someone was already brewing coffee. Somewhere in the distance, a rooster crowed—Key West's unofficial alarm clock. She made her way into Old Town, weaving around a trash truck and a cyclist who gave her a sleepy wave. She didn't wave back.

Her mind was still stuck in the dream—no, the nightmare—its imagery burned into her brain like an afterimage from staring too long at the sun. The way the bodies had looked. The way the music had reversed itself. The hum. Rachel's lifeless face. The rope. The words.

She parked her moped at the curb near Shrimp Boat

Sound and cut the engine. It was quiet there, still tucked away from the hustle of Duval Street. The courtyard behind the studio was shaded and still, surrounded by flowering bushes and a rusting metal fence. She found her usual bench near the old bougainvillea and sat, letting her arms rest on her thighs, hands dangling between her knees.

Silence.

Save for another rooster crowing off in the distance, the world felt paused. She liked this spot.

She had come here with Rachel back when Rachel was still trying to decide if she wanted to move full-time to the island. They'd split a cinnamon roll and coffee on that bench, and Rachel had said she liked the way this place felt—like it wasn't trying too hard to be anything it wasn't. Now she was dead. Strangled, staged, left to rot under a moonlit sky with a piece of fucking driftwood at her feet like some sick calling card.

Pati ran her hands through her hair, tugging lightly at the roots. Danny was still lying to her. That much was clear. Sure, he'd admitted to being in the Keys earlier than he claimed, but that only raised more questions. Why not tell her the truth from the beginning? Why show up now, like a ghost from a failed marriage, conveniently when things were unraveling?

And that song. She heard "La Vie en Rose" at the bonfire, someone was humming it. She thought it was Michel, but what if it wasn't? Danny had been listening to it—crying to it—like it was the only thing tethering him to the world. She could drive herself mad with theories. Maybe she already was. But what she did know, sitting there with her heart thudding against her ribs, was that she couldn't wait for someone else to figure it out.

Not the cops. Not even Nate. She thought about that first body in Islamorada. The second in Marathon. Then Stock Island. Higgs Beach. Fort Zachary. Five women. And all this time, she'd been too busy bartending and babysitting her mess of a brother-in-law to connect the dots.

But it was connected. She felt it in her bones. Something was tying them all together—some pattern, some logic that hadn't fully revealed itself yet. The rope. The driftwood. The setting. Always by water. Always posed.

And always—always—a message.

The island was full of ghosts now. Not the rattling-chains kind, but the kind that lingered in the corner of your mind when you walked down familiar streets. The kind that made you hesitate when a stranger smiled at you in passing. The kind that made moonlight feel like a warning. She leaned back against the bench and tilted her head toward the sky. The stars were fading, but one or two still clung to the navy-blue horizon, refusing to let go.

"Okay," she whispered to herself. If no one else was going to find the killer, she would. She didn't care how crazy it sounded. She'd been on this island too long not to trust her instincts. And they were screaming now. Screaming at her that time was running out. That whoever was doing this wasn't finished. She took a deep breath, the salt air catching in her throat.

With or without Nate's help, she was going to figure this out. One way or another.

By 7:30, the sun had climbed just high enough to start warming the courtyard. The shadows were pulling back, the first wave of delivery trucks grumbled down White Street, and the rooster chorus had calmed to the occasional soloist. Pati pulled her phone from her bag and stared at the screen, thumb hovering.

Was 7:30 too early?

She thought about the dream again. About Rachel. About that driftwood, carved like a promise or a warning. About Danny's tear-streaked face and the voice in her dream saying she couldn't protect anyone. She pressed send before she could talk herself out of it.

Pati: *Hey. Sorry it's early. Any new info?*

The response came quicker than she expected.

Nate: *You heard already?*

Pati: *Heard…?*

Her stomach dropped. Was there another victim?

Nate: *There was another attack. Well, attempted. She got away.*

Pati's eyes grew huge as she read the text. Word got around fast on the island—even faster when the words were strung together like: someone escaped the French-man killer. It wouldn't be long before everyone knew, but right now, she felt like she was on the inside of the investigation–exactly where she wanted to be.

Pati: *What happened?*

There was a long pause. The typing dots came and went twice. She imagined him pacing, phone in one hand, trying to figure out what he could tell her without violating some protocol.

Finally: Nate: *We're with her now.*

Pati's heart skipped.

Pati: *Holy shit. She okay?*

Nate: *Banged up. Shaken. But alive. EMTs evaluated her, but we've got herm, and we're heading back to the scene now.*

Pati's skin prickled.

Pati: *Did she see him?*

Nate: *She thinks she got a good look.*

Pati: *Where did this happen?*

Nate: *I figured that's why you knew. Not far from your place, by Hogfish.*

Before Pati could reply, another message from Nate: *We've got it taped off. CSI is on the way. We're doing a canvas.*

And then a third, as if he could read her mind. Nate: *Don't come.*

Pati scoffed out loud.

Pati: *You really think I'm not going to come?*

Nate: *I know you. But I have to say it anyway.*

She didn't reply right away. Her fingers tightened around the phone, knuckles pale. Someone had survived. That changed everything. Not just for the case, but for her. It meant the killer was sloppy. Or maybe unraveling. And if he was unraveling, she could catch him. She could stop this before it happened again.

Pati looked up from her phone. The sun was climbing higher, painting streaks of gold across the wall behind the studio. Her heart thudded behind her ribs like it had somewhere to be. She stood up, slid her phone into her back pocket, and headed for the moped.

Nate could yell at her later. Right now, she had work to do.

CHAPTER 16
DRIFTWOOD CASTLE

The engine sputtered once, coughed like an old smoker, then caught with a growl that felt too loud for the sleepy courtyard. She didn't care.

The streets were still mostly quiet. Too early for the brunch crowd, too late for the bakers. A few locals were out tending their gardens, waving at each other over low fences. She saw a guy in board shorts and flip-flops walking a tiny dog that looked like a wet sock. A woman in an oversized sunhat was unlocking a café door and pulling in a crate of papayas.

Pati kept her eyes forward. She zoomed past chickens pecking and bobbing through a gravel alleyway, their feathers catching the golden morning light. One darted into the road and she swerved, cursing under her breath but not slowing down.

She opened up the throttle fully and merged onto US Route 1—now officially renamed the Jimmy Buffett Memorial Highway. The new green road sign gleamed in the sun, freshly installed and not yet faded by salt or storms.

She might've cracked a smile at it any other day. Today, she didn't even blink.

The moped ate up the short ride over the bridge back to Stock Island, the water glittering on either side, calm and indifferent. Her heart pounded—not from the ride, but from the certainty in her gut. She was close. To something. Maybe the killer. Maybe just another piece of the puzzle. But she wasn't letting this trail go cold.

She turned onto Front Street and everything looked deceptively normal. The soft hum of a window AC unit rattled behind a bungalow. Palm fronds stirred lazily overhead. A lawn sprinkler hissed in even bursts, ticking like a metronome as it swung side to side. It was the normalcy that made Pati's skin crawl.

To her left, the quiet back side of her neighborhood lay just beyond the mangroves and scrubby patches of grass. Some homes backed right up to the water; others clustered together, colorful clapboard boxes in an unspoken community. This was her turf. Her shortcuts. Her corner stores and porch-sitting neighbors.

That's what got her.

This wasn't just Stock Island anymore. This was home.

And Hogfish wasn't just another dive bar. It was her sanctuary—the one bar in the Keys she didn't ever work in. She could belly up to the weathered bar, kick her flip-flops off, and let someone else pour the damn drink. And now? It felt tainted.

As she rounded the bend, her eyes scanned the side

of the road out of habit. That's when she saw it—something odd, just off the shoulder where the dirt path cut across the grass.

There was no sidewalk there. Never had been. Just a patch of crabgrass and sand where locals had worn their own trail from the street into the neighborhood. Pati had walked it a hundred times. Biked it. Run across it in the rain. The shortcut was second nature.

Which is why the lump on the path stood out. She eased off the throttle and coasted toward it. The moped's low growl purred in the still air as she crossed to the wrong side of the road, then slowed to a stop on the shoulder. It was a piece of driftwood. No question. Weathered and sanded down by coral and sea. Rounded edges. A warm, pale gray like a bone left too long in the sun.

She flipped up the kickstand but didn't kill the engine. Some part of her didn't want to stay long. She crouched beside it, her fingers brushing the smooth surface of the front. Nothing obvious at first glance. But then her thumb traced something—subtle ridges, a slight indentation.

She turned it over.

The back was rougher. Still smooth from tumbling through tide and time, but grooved. Carved. Three words. By the light. The rest of the phrase was missing. No "of the moon." No "it'll be all right." Just the beginning. An echo of a message unfinished. Her stomach dropped. This wasn't driftwood anymore. It was a breadcrumb. The killer had been here. Maybe hours ago. Maybe less.

And he'd dropped this—what? Accidentally? Deliberately? Had he meant to finish the carving? Had something interrupted him? Pati didn't wait to find out.

She tucked the driftwood under her arm, pivoted on her heel, and jumped back on the moped in one smooth motion. Gravel crunched beneath the tires as she spun it around, pointing it straight toward the Hogfish Bar and the cluster of crime scene tape ahead.

The engine whined as she revved hard, kicking up a plume of dust behind her. The unfinished message burned in her chest. She'd been chasing clues for days, following whispers and shadows. But this? This was real. Physical. Something she could hold in her hands.

By the time Pati pulled up near the scene, the air was already heavy with heat and tension. The police tape fluttered in the breeze, sectioning off the gravel path behind Hogfish like it was a movie set. A couple of officers stood around talking in low tones, hands on hips, sunglasses perched with all the performative calm of people trying to keep a lid on chaos.

Pati cut the engine and swung her leg off the moped. She didn't even get a full step in before Nate was on her.

"Pati, no. I told you not to come."

She ignored him, reaching under her arm and pulling

out the driftwood. She didn't wave it. She tossed it at his chest like a gauntlet. He caught it, stumbling slightly.

"Jesus," he muttered, looking down.

"I found it on the cut-through," she said. "You know the one. Between Front and the neighborhood. Just lying there. And yeah, I picked it up. Sorry for contaminating your precious evidence, but I wasn't exactly gonna leave it for the chickens."

He flipped it over in his hands, saw the words.

By the light.

His eyes flicked up to her, but she was already talking again.

"I live up the fucking street, Nate. This is my neighborhood. My people. My friends. That girl—Rachel—she was my friend. And now this?"

"Don't you think I understand that?" he snapped, more tired than angry. "This is my home too."

"Then let me help." Her voice cracked just enough to let some of the raw undercurrent show. "Let me do something. I can't just sit at home while women are dying in my backyard."

Nate pinched the bridge of his nose, exhaling hard.

"I get it. I do. But this isn't—"

Before he could finish, an unmarked black SUV rolled up slowly to the edge of the scene. It pulled in tight against the curb and stopped with a soft crunch of tires against gravel. The driver's side door opened, and out stepped Detective Trent Morillo, tall and stone-faced, his gray shirt rolled at the elbows and his hair slicked back like he'd just stepped out of an old noir film.

He rounded the vehicle and opened the passenger door.

Pati's breath caught when she saw the girl step out.

She couldn't have been more than twenty-two. Brown hair, blue eyes. A lightweight hoodie zipped halfway up over a tank top. She looked like she could've been headed to class or coffee with friends, not recovering from an attempted murder. Her face was pale, but calm—too calm.

Pati's chest twisted. The girl could've been a younger version of Clara. That familiar jawline, the same stubborn set to her mouth. It was like looking at a parallel life, one where her sister had taken a different path. She suddenly understood why survivors hated the word "lucky."

The pair began walking toward them, slow and steady. Nate turned to intercept them.

But Pati stepped forward without thinking, her voice shooting out before she could stop herself.

"Are you the survivor?"

The girl paused mid-step. Trent stopped walking too, frowning slightly.

Nate turned sharply toward Pati, his mouth open.

She knew, immediately, that it wasn't her place to ask. Not like that. Not in the middle of a taped-off scene with three grown men standing between her and the worst night of that girl's life. Clara would've cringed. Hell, Pati cringed. She could practically hear her sister's voice in her head already—Pati, for god's sake, learn some grace. But instead of recoiling, the girl let out a breath that sounded dangerously close to a chuckle. She gave a half-smile, soft and strange.

"Yeah," she said, her voice hoarse but steady. "I guess so."

The simplicity of it hit Pati like a slap. Not a victim. Not a witness. Not even a name. Just the survivor.

Trent's voice cut the moment. "We're here to do a walkthrough. See if anything else comes back to her now that she's had a few hours to rest."

Pati stood still, mouth suddenly dry.

"I'm sorry," she said, directing it to the girl, not the cops. "I didn't mean to ambush you."

The girl nodded, her expression unreadable. "You didn't. It's fine. I've heard worse."

Trent turned back to Nate. "You coming?"

Nate hesitated for half a second, then passed the driftwood to one of the officers and gave Pati a long, hard look.

Trent and the girl turned toward the dock, and Nate followed. The yellow tape fluttered back into place as they ducked under.

Pati stood tiptoed behind them, hoping they simply wouldn't notice she was following them beyond the tape, and suddenly feeling the weight of the sun and the sweat gathering at the back of her neck. She hadn't realized until now that her hands were shaking again. Her stomach roiled with guilt and curiosity and something else—something closer to fury.

Whoever this man was, he'd done this again. And again. And again. He'd left his eerie calling cards, tied their wrists like some sick mockery of prayer, and hunted them like ghosts slipping through mangroves.

And now, he'd nearly succeeded again.

Except this time, someone got away.

And that changed everything.

Pati had followed them under the tape like a shadow—quiet, steady, pretending like she belonged. She stayed a few paces back, eyes wide, feet deliberately silent on the packed gravel path. She figured if she didn't speak, maybe no one would notice. Or maybe no one would stop her. Nate and Trent were busy leading the girl toward the far end of the dock, murmuring something low, something procedural.

But then Nate glanced over his shoulder.

Caught.

His eyes landed on her. There was a flicker of frustration, but also something else—resignation, maybe. He didn't motion for her to leave. Didn't even sigh. Just turned back around and said something quietly to Trent, who twisted to look at her with narrowed eyes. The kind of look that said: *This is a police investigation, not a gossip tour.*

Pati gave a little shrug, held her ground. She wasn't going anywhere.

The girl turned around then too, curious. She looked worn around the edges from the night, but sharp-eyed. She saw Pati immediately and tilted her head.

"Who's she?" the girl asked, jabbing a thumb in Pati's direction.

"She's…" Nate started, but didn't finish.

"I'm the one who found the driftwood that was probably meant for you," Pati said, again wishing she had the tact of her sister.

"Yeah and honestly, I really wish you had just told us about that instead of contaminating our crime scene," Trent interjected.

Pati rolled her eyes and mustered a "sorry."

"Listen," the girl said. "Can I just tell you what happened?"

"That would be great," Trent said.

So she did.

"I was at Hogfish last night," she began, folding her arms. "Drinks with some friends. One of them has a boat docked nearby, so we went back there, hung out a little more. Smoked, played cards, got loud. You know how it is. Everyone else was crashing on the boat, but I was staying at a B&B nearby and I wanted my own bed. So I started walking back." She shrugged. "Wasn't even that late. Maybe 2? 2:30?"

Pati nodded, listening closely.

"And that's when I saw him. At first, I thought he was just another guy out for a walk. He had this wine bottle in his hand—unopened. Like, who brings an unopened bottle of wine for a solo stroll? Red wine, too. I'm not a snob or anything, but that's just weird."

"What kind of wine?" Pati asked.

"Beaujolais," the girl said without hesitation. "Pretty sure. Bright red writing on the label. I took sommelier classes last year, and I spent a summer in Beaujolais. Worked a vineyard. I know that bottle. It looked like a Domaine Les Charmes. Not something you just stumble across at a gas station."

Pati raised her eyebrows. "And the accent?"

"Oh my God," the girl said, laughing once, sharp and bitter. "That was the worst part. He was trying to sound suave. Like *suave* suave. 'Chérie' this and 'ma belle' that. But the rhythm was all wrong. It was like a knockoff perfume. Sounded French, but didn't feel French, you know?"

Nate muttered, "We've heard that before."

"He didn't think it was bad," she continued. "He was so confident about it, like he'd practiced. He even did that thing where you squint and tilt your head like you're about to whisper poetry."

Pati grimaced. "Gross."

"Oh, super gross. And then he stepped toward me, all smooth-like, reaching out with this weird, lazy grin. But I wasn't drunk. I smoke more than I drink, and I didn't even finish my last beer. So I dodged him. Bolted. He shouted something behind me, but I didn't turn back."

"Did he chase you?" Trent asked, his voice clipped.

"No," she said, serious now. "I don't think so. I ran fast, and there was a car coming around the bend with headlights on. I think that spooked him. When I looked back, he was gone."

"Did you see where he went?"

She shook her head. "No. But he was barefoot. That part I remember because I thought, what kind of creeper tries to kidnap someone barefoot?"

Pati laughed, just a little. Couldn't help it.

"He was close," the girl said then, her voice suddenly soft. "Like, too close. He knew that shortcut path. He was waiting."

Pati shivered. That worn dirt path she crossed every week. The shortcut everyone used because the sidewalks were broken or didn't exist. That was her neighborhood. Her backyard.

She caught Nate looking at her again. There was something like an apology in his eyes. Or maybe it was guilt for ever thinking he could keep her out of this.

She didn't speak, but the words were loud in her bones: This is my island, too.

The girl, whose name Pati eventually learned was Rae, kept walking, and the three of them followed her.

"You know it's weird you found driftwood," Rae said. "He kept saying something about taking me to his driftwood castle."

"That has to be directly connected to the driftwood found at each scene," Nate said.

"No shit, Sherlock," Rae quipped, earning a suppressed smile out of Detective Morillo.

Pati was surprised at how forthcoming this young woman was. She was young, but she seemed pretty unfazed at having been the near victim of a serial killer.

"You seem pretty calm for all you've been through," Pati finally said aloud.

"I guess I have to laugh," Rae said. "If I couldn't laugh, I'd just go insane." She shrugged her shoulders.

In an effort to get the discussion back on track, the detective spoke up.

"So where exactly did he come from? Or when did you notice him first?" Trent asked.

"Ya know," Rae pondered the question for a minute. "I didn't actually see him first. I heard him."

"Heard him?" Trent probed.

"Yeah, he was humming something," Rae said. She tried to replicate the noise she heard. It was crude and not quite there, but Pati recognized it immediately. Trent and Nate were still listening closely to Rae's impromptu performance when Pati blurted it out.

"It's 'La Vie en Rose.'"

Goosebumps stood out on Pati's arms despite the morning sun. A sudden realization hit her in the chest, and before anyone could ask further questions, Pati spat out, "I've got to go." She ran to her moped and took off up the street, back toward home.

CHAPTER 17
THE THINGS WE DON'T SAY

Pati's moped sped down Front Street, and her stomach churned. She kept telling herself she had to get home, but before she knew it, she felt nauseous, like vomit was imminent. She slammed on the breaks and jumped off the moped, leaving it running on its side. Heaving into the grass, she notices she's exactly by the makeshift path leading into her neighborhood—precisely where she found the driftwood earlier that morning.

She took a deep breath, trying to steady herself. Turning onto her back, she felt the grass and the gravel underneath her. She looked up at the sky, the gulls flying overhead. Island life hadn't stopped, so why did it feel like her heart was about to?

She didn't move. Couldn't. But her hand slipped into her pocket almost on instinct, finding her phone by touch. She unlocked it with a thumb swipe and hesitated over the contacts list. Clara.

Pati's thumb hovered. They hadn't spoken since… since before. Way before. Before the murders. Before Danny showed up. Before everything cracked.

She hit "Call" before she could talk herself out of it.

It rang once. Twice.

"Pati?"

Clara's voice came through soft and cautious, like she hadn't expected to ever hear from her again.

"Clara. Hi, yeah, it's me."

There was a pause, the inevitable awkwardness that comes with randomly calling a mildly estranged sibling and having them actually pick up.

"It's good to hear from you," Clara said.

"How are things? How are you?" Pati asked.

"Well, I—" Clara's voice cracked. Pati could hear a muffled sniffle. "I guess things are not so great right now."

Pati squeezed her eyes shut. Her voice came out ragged. "I'm sorry," she whispered. "I should've called. I—I didn't know what to say."

There was a pause on the other end, then a shaky inhale. "I thought you were mad at me."

"I was," Pati admitted. "But not about you. About… everything. I don't even know anymore."

She heard Clara exhale.

"Well," Clara said carefully, "I'm not mad. But I am scared."

That stopped Pati cold.

"Scared?" she repeated. "Clara, what—?"

"It's Danny," Clara said, voice tight. "I didn't know how to explain it before. I thought maybe if he left for a while, things would cool off. But he's not well,

Pati. He hasn't been for a long time. And I don't know where he is."

Pati sat up slowly, dust sticking to the sweat on her back.

"What do you mean 'not well'?"

There was silence for a beat too long.

"He sees things," Clara said finally. "That aren't there. He hears things. It started small—just confusion, forgetfulness. Then it turned into full-scale delusions. He started speaking French out of nowhere, quoting poetry he never used to know, and drinking wine like he thought he was someone else. And then he wouldn't remember the episodes at all. He kept saying he wanted to rekindle things between us… like when we were younger. But…" Her voice cracked. "I haven't felt that way about Danny in years. He's not that person anymore. He's angry, Pati. Drunk. Sometimes cruel."

Pati's stomach turned again.

She dug her nails into her thigh. Hard.

"How long has this been happening?"

"Longer than I'd like to admit," Clara said softly. "But it got worse this past year. He lost his job. He stopped talking to friends. It's like he's built this version of our life in his head that never actually existed. He was seeing a doctor for a while when it first started, but then he decided the medication made him less 'him' and stopped it cold turkey."

Pati's breath came short and shallow. Her eyes darted to the street, then back toward the moped lying on its side like a broken toy.

"Oh fuck," she muttered.

"What?"

"Clara," she said, her voice barely audible, "Danny's *here.*"

Silence.

"He's…he's been here. He's staying at my place. Sleeping on my couch. He said you two were just going through a rough patch. I thought… I don't know what I thought. But he didn't seem—"

"Dangerous?" Clara's voice cut in, sharper now. "He doesn't seem dangerous. That's the problem. But it's like something's rotting inside him and he's just barely keeping the lid on. You have no idea how good he is at hiding it. He's… he's manipulative. He's been isolating me for years."

Pati pressed her free hand to her forehead.

"I let him in," she whispered. "Clara, I let him into my home."

Another long silence stretched between them, the air buzzing in Pati's ear.

"I'm sorry," Clara said eventually, and Pati knew she meant it in more ways than one.

The weight of it hit her all at once.

"La Vie en Rose." The wine. The fake accent. The "driftwood castle." The Frenchman.

Danny.

"Oh my god," Pati breathed. "Oh my god."

Her legs trembled as she stood up. The grass clung to her shirt. She dusted herself off mechanically, the phone still pressed to her ear. The wind stirred again, blowing a few stray palm fronds across the yard beside her. Everything looked so normal. She stared at the dirt path, now forever altered. A crime scene, retroactively. A breadcrumb trail that had been under her nose for days. For years, maybe.

"Clara?"

"Yeah?"

"I'm sorry I didn't see it sooner."

"I'm sorry I let it get this far."

They exchanged shaky breaths. Then Clara broke the silence.

"I need to get on a plane," she said, voice rising. "I need to come down there. Today."

"That's probably a good idea," Pati replied, barely above a whisper. "Because I think Danny is in some deep shit."

"How deep?"

Pati stood, brushed the gravel off her hands, and swallowed hard.

"I think he's hurt people."

There was a pause.

"Clara," she said. "I think he's killed them."

The silence that followed was so dense it felt like the air around her changed.

"No," Clara said finally. But it didn't sound like denial. It sounded like grief. Like her body couldn't keep up with the truth. "I mean," she whispered, "I knew he wasn't well. But murder? I just—I didn't think he could—"

"I wouldn't either," Pati said. "But I've been chasing

ghosts for days. A fake Frenchman, wine bottles, staged crime scenes. A girl nearly died last night. And he's been right here. Sleeping in my fucking living room."

Clara's voice dropped into a low, fearful register.

"He was drinking more. Way more. And the delusions—he stopped calling them that. He started believing them. He said he was reclaiming his past. That we'd lost something sacred. He wanted to be the man I fell in love with, only—he's not that man anymore. Hasn't been for years."

Pati could hear the tremble in her sister's voice now. She knew that fear. The kind you try to out-reason until it's staring you down.

"Is this why we haven't spoken? Why didn't you tell me sooner?" she asked.

Clara gave a hollow laugh.

"Because I was embarrassed. Because he convinced me I was overreacting. Because I was tired. I don't know. Pick one."

Pati let out a breath, paced a few feet along the grass. A rusty mailbox rattled in the breeze beside her.

"I'm scared of him," Clara said softly. "But I never thought he'd actually kill someone."

Pati stared down the makeshift path—sunlight dappled over the place the driftwood had been.

"Well," she said, "you might've underestimated him."

"I'm booking the flight," Clara said. "I'll text you once it's confirmed."

"Text me from the airport. Don't go home. Don't tell anyone where you're going. And Clara?"

"Yeah?"

"I'm really sorry."

"I am too."

They hung up.

Pati laid there for a second, phone still in hand, screen gone dark. A soft breeze tugged at her shirt. Somewhere nearby, a rooster crowed. Her mouth was dry, her heart hammering like it had nowhere left to hide.

She tried to breathe, but everything felt thin. Off-kilter. *What the fuck do I do now?* She stared at the sun-baked gravel under her feet, trying to make sense of any of it. How had she not seen it? The long quiet looks. The wine. The soft humming. La Vie en Rose.

Had it always been there, waiting for her to notice? She tilted her head to the side and pressed her cheek to her knee. *If he is the Frenchman… then he's been playing me this whole time. And if he wasn't? Then the killer was still out there, and she'd just lit a match to her own family. Neither version felt survivable.*

She squeezed her eyes shut and counted to ten. Nothing changed when she opened them again. The street was still quiet. The moped still lay on its side like a warning. She didn't move. Not yet.

For the first time since the murders began, she realized she wasn't just following a mystery. She was part of it. And someone she loved might be the monster at the center of it.

CHAPTER 18
TIDAL PULL

The moped's wheels clicked quietly as Pati walked it the rest of the way down the cut-through path. She was only a minute from home. A minute from the couch where Danny was—hopefully—still sleeping. A minute from her old life, her normal routine, the illusion that the worst thing in her house might be dust or overdue bills. But now, each step felt like walking into the mouth of something she couldn't see.

She kept glancing over her shoulder. The path curved slightly between two lots of overgrown brush and low fencing. She could hear a sprinkler hissing in the next yard. Could hear birdsong. Could feel the pulse of her heartbeat in her ears.

She had trusted him. Danny had been her make-shift family for years—sitting on her porch, eating late-night conch fritters, talking music, heartbreak, nothing and everything. He never once made her feel unsafe. Even when he drank too much. Even when he got quiet and strange. But if Clara was telling the truth—if the delusions were real, if the accent and the wine weren't just an affectation but a signal—then who was he? And what the hell was he capable of? She stopped at the corner and breathed in deep, the kind of breath you take before diving under a wave. Then she turned onto her block.

Her front porch looked the same as always. Her windchimes danced a little in the breeze. Her beach chair was still angled toward the street like it always was—Pati's perch for late-night people-watching. And beyond the porch, her front door, still closed, still unassuming.

She walked the moped into the yard and leaned it against the fence. Her keys felt sharp in her hand as she slid them into the lock.

Click. The door creaked open.

Inside, the air was cooler. Dim. Her curtains were drawn. The place smelled faintly like coffee and sunscreen and something sharper—red wine. She stepped in slowly, quiet as a shadow.

There he was. Danny. Sprawled on the couch like he always did, one arm over his eyes, one bare foot hanging off the edge. Snoring lightly. He hadn't stirred. He looked almost childlike in sleep, mouth parted slightly, chest rising and falling in a slow, even rhythm.

He looked harmless.

Pati froze.

Was she really about to accuse this man—this man, the one who made her birthday playlists and once patched a leak in her roof with a tarp and duct tape—of murder?

She didn't move. Couldn't. She stood there in the doorway between the kitchen and the living room, watching him sleep, heart clattering in her chest.

She had done this before—jumped to conclusions. She'd practically led the pitchfork parade against Michel. She'd stirred up suspicion and tension. Made people second-guess themselves. Nate had second-guessed himself because of her. And Michel had turned out to be exactly what he said he was: odd, intense, annoying—but not a killer.

Was she just doing it again? Was her brain, frayed from days without sleep and stories without answers, just looking for someone to blame? She wanted so badly for that to be true. But Clara had sounded scared and serious. Not exasperated. Not vengeful. Not fed up. Afraid. And Clara didn't do fear easily. Her sister was the composed one. The rational one. She didn't spin stories. She didn't exaggerate. And she certainly didn't say things like "delusions" and "he started speaking French" and "he becomes someone I don't know" unless something was very wrong.

This wasn't paranoia. This wasn't a hunch. It was a pattern. A trail of crumbs. The same wine. The same song. The same shift in personality that Clara had described. And he was here. Right here. What could she do? Wake him up and ask point-blank: Did you kill them?

Call Nate? Call Trent? Tell them her hunch—again— and hope they'd believe her this time? She'd lost credibility with them after Michel. She knew it. She could see it in their eyes every time she opened her mouth. If she was wrong again, she'd lose them completely. But if she was right and she didn't say something…more women could die. Her palms were damp. She flexed her fingers, then clenched them again. Danny let out a soft snort in his sleep and rolled to one side. Pati flinched.

She backed up slowly to the counter, her eyes never leaving him. From here, she could see the whole room. The door. Her phone. A frying pan. She didn't want to need a weapon. She didn't want this to be real. But she wasn't sure she had the luxury of denial anymore. She crossed her arms tight over her chest and stood there. Watching him sleep. Just thinking. *What the hell do I do now?*

Danny slept like he hadn't a care in the world. The way his arm flopped over his stomach, the light whistle of his breath—if you didn't know better, you'd think he was just some overgrown beach bum who passed out after too many mojitos. Not someone who might've killed multiple women.

Her stomach flipped. Her phone buzzed on the counter. Nate: *What the hell was that? Everything OK?*

She swiped the message away with a flick of her thumb—she couldn't answer him yet. Not until she knew what she was doing. Instead, she opened a new message thread. Her fingers hovered over the keyboard for a second, then typed: Clara. The name popped up instantly, but what caught her off guard was the thread history. There wasn't any. Not for a year. Just a single message from Clara, green-bubbled and curt: *You do what you want, Pati. I'm done trying.* No response from Pati. That was the last thing they'd said to each other.

Pati closed her eyes, guilt burning behind her eyelids like a fever. She'd been so quick to blame Clara for the rift between them. Told herself that Clara had chosen a boring life, that she'd gotten uptight, cold. Pati had convinced herself that it was Clara who'd changed. But maybe it wasn't that simple. Maybe Danny had been working his slow erosion all along. Isolating Clara not just from friends and neighbors, but from her. And Pati—blind, trusting, loyal to a fault—had let him. Had become part of it. And now she was harboring her sister's clinically delusional husband. Ex-husband? That part she still didn't know. Clara hadn't said. Were they even legally separated? Divorced? Had she filed papers? Had she tried? But that didn't matter right now. Her fingers flew across the screen. *Are you seriously coming down here??*

The response came less than a minute later.

Yes. My flight leaves at 3 p.m. I expect to land at 7:35.

Classic Clara. Punctual. Precise. Efficient in a way that made her feel vaguely robotic and vaguely terrifying. Even in the face of possible homicide, she still typed like she was filing a quarterly report. Pati stared at the screen, thumbs hovering. There was a question she wanted to ask. Needed to ask. But even now, she hesitated. Like asking it would make this all more real.

Finally, she typed: *Do you want me to wait for you to*

get here? Or should I notify the authorities?

She barely had time to breathe before the reply came in: *Fuck no. The next time I see him, he better be in custody.*

Pati blinked. Clara didn't swear. Not even when their dog died in high school. Not even when one of Danny's friends got too drunk at the wedding. If Clara was swearing now, she wasn't just scared. She was done. Pati sighed and set the phone down. She circled the counter slowly, like she was approaching a sleeping tiger instead of the man who'd once helped her fix her porch fan without being asked.

Danny was still sprawled on the couch, mouth open slightly, arms thrown wide like he owned the room. The sound of his snoring grated now—nasal and rhythmic and totally oblivious. She stopped at the edge of the coffee table, took one more breath, and raised her phone. *Click.* One photo. Slightly angled. Caught him mid-snore. He looked so normal it made her stomach twist. She backed away, opened Nate's message thread, and dropped the photo in. Her thumb hovered. She shouldn't be hesitating. Not now. Clara had confirmed it. The erratic behavior. The delusions. The French affectation that wasn't just some wine-soaked quirk—it was a symptom. A signpost pointing to something darker. But why did this feel like betrayal?

Because it wasn't just that he was her sister's husband. It was that Danny got her. Or at least she thought he had. The late nights spent dissecting music lyrics over beer and grilled pineapple. The long talks about grief and not fitting in. The way he always understood when she said she felt like an outsider, even in her own life. If he saw her that clearly—and he was a killer—then what did that say about her? Did she share something in common with someone capable of that kind of violence? Her finger trembled over the screen. She shook her head. It doesn't matter. She clicked into the message box, typing slowly. *Ask Rae if this is the man who came after her last night?*

Then she hit send. It felt like crossing a line she couldn't come back from. She stared at the screen for a beat, but no dots appeared. She turned her phone over and pressed it to her chest. Danny shifted and let out a groggy sigh. Pati stiffened. He didn't wake, just scratched his chest, rolled onto his side, and resumed snoring like nothing had changed. But everything had changed.

She took a step back, her mind racing with possibilities. *If Rae recognized him, Nate would act. There'd be no going back.* She'd be part of the investigation now, whether they wanted her or not. And if Rae didn't recognize him…

Well. She didn't know what that meant. Yet.

Her phone buzzed again. She snatched it up, half expecting it to be Nate with Rae's answer. But it was Clara again. *Just promise me you'll be careful. If he's off his meds—or never had any to begin with—you don't know what version of him you'll get when he wakes up.*

Pati read it three times. Then looked across the room

at the version of him she had right now: the snoring one. The innocent one. The mask. What happens when it slips?

She closed her eyes and tried to breathe. Everything was in motion now.

The tide had shifted.

And Pati—caught in the pull—wasn't sure if she was finally about to reach solid ground or get dragged out to sea.

CHAPTER 19
THE FRENCHMAN

Pati's chest was heavy as she stared at her phone, waiting. The photo hung in the thread like a loaded question.

Text bubbles appeared. Then disappeared. Then came back again.

She held her breath. Her heartbeat thudded in her ears. When the reply finally came through, it wasn't at all what she expected: *WTF, Pati.*

She blinked. Seriously? Then her phone started ringing—startling her so hard she nearly dropped it, even though it was already in her hand and she'd been staring at the screen. She glanced toward the couch. Danny was still snoring, arm now over his forehead like he was shielding his eyes from the truth. She tiptoed to the front door, slipped out, and pulled it closed behind her with as little sound as possible.

"Hello?" she answered.

Nate's voice hissed through the line, tight and sharp. "Who the hell is that, and where the hell are you, and what the hell is going on?"

Pati exhaled.

"I'm home," she said quietly. "That's my brother-in-law. Or… ex–brother-in-law, I suppose. And he's asleep on my couch."

A pause. "Your what?"

"His name's Danny," she said. "Clara's… ex. Or maybe not officially. I don't know. He's my sister's husband. Or was."

"And you think he attacked Rae last night?" Nate asked, voice thick with disbelief. "Did you see him leave? Did he come home wet, bloodied, suspicious—anything?"

"No," Pati admitted. "We got into a fight. He was drinking heavily—a red wine. I went to bed and passed out. He could've left and come back. Hogfish isn't far. You know that."

There was a long exhale on the other end.

"Pati," Nate said slowly, "that sounds extremely circumstantial. I get that you feel oblig—"

"I called Clara," Pati interrupted. Her voice was low but firm. "I didn't just wake up with a bad feeling and decide to point fingers. I called my sister, Nate. She flat out told me he's delusional. Clinically diagnosed. She said the delusions get worse when he drinks. She said he starts acting like someone else."

She swallowed, steadying herself.

"She said he started speaking French. Drinking Beaujolais. Said he wanted to 'rekindle their love' like they were still twenty-something lovers in Paris. But Clara hasn't felt that way about him in years. She said he's not just mentally ill, Nate—he's abusive. He isolated her. He made her think she was the problem. And now—" Her throat tightened. "Now he's here. Sleeping like he hasn't done a damn thing."

The line went quiet. When Nate spoke again, his voice was softer. "Well… damn, Pati. I don't really know what to say to that."

Pati leaned against her porch railing. Her fingers were trembling around the phone. "I feel guilty," she admitted. "For not seeing it sooner. I let him in. I defended him. I was so fixated on Michel and his weird accent and that stupid jukebox obsession that I didn't even notice…"

Her voice trailed.

"All the victims," she said after a pause, "they look like Clara."

That hung there. Heavy and unanswerable.

"You think it's intentional?" Nate finally asked.

"I think it's personal," Pati replied. "Which is worse."

Another silence. Then: "Do you have his DNA?" Nate asked. "We can compare it to the sample we pulled from the second crime scene."

"Not directly," she said, glancing toward her front door. "But I'm sure I could find something. Razor, glass, toothbrush…"

She straightened, then hesitated. "Did you guys ever find that wine bottle Rae mentioned? The Beaujolais?"

"No," Nate said. "We think he brought it home with him. Can you check if it's there?"

Pati frowned. "I didn't see a bottle out—but I'll look again."

"Okay. Hang tight. Morillo and I are on our way."

The line went dead.

Pati lowered the phone slowly, staring out at the quiet street. Her block was calm, sun-drenched, like it had no idea what was happening inside her house. She tucked the phone in her pocket and took one last breath of clean air before easing the front door open and slipping back inside.

Danny was still out cold, snoring just a bit louder now, one hand splayed across his chest. She crept past him and into the kitchen, scanning the counters. No wine bottle.

She checked the trash. Nothing. Then she crouched to open the cabinet under the sink—where she sometimes tossed recycling when the bin outside was full. Not there either.

She approached the living room again. Danny stirred. She held her breath. But as she passed the coffee table, something dark glinted from beneath the couch. She crouched, tilting her head toward it. There it was. The bottle.

It must have slipped from Danny's hand while he was sleeping—rolled quietly under the edge of the couch, where her vacuum rarely reached. She crouched lower, bracing herself with one hand and reaching for it with the other. Her fingers closed around the neck of the bottle, smooth and cold. Domaine Les Charmes. The label was exactly what Rae described.

As she pulled back, her head cracked against the bottom of the coffee table with a thunk loud enough to wake the dead.

"Shit—ow!" she yelped.

And just like that, Danny awoke.

"Whoa—hey!" he said, startled. His voice was hoarse with sleep. He blinked and sat up halfway. "Pati? What the hell—are you okay?"

She whipped around on her knees, bottle still in hand, heart hammering in her chest.

"Yeah! Sorry," she said, voice too bright, too fast. "Just, uh, saw this bottle and wanted to clean it up before it got knocked over." That was a lame excuse, she thought to herself, considering she found it knocked over. Danny rubbed his eyes and looked down at the bottle.

"Oh," he said. "Right. Must've dropped it."

She offered a tight smile. The kind of smile you wear when you're face-to-face with someone who might be a serial killer, and you're still not totally sure whether they even know they're a serial killer.

"Yeah, no worries," she said, her voice trembling at the edges despite her best efforts to keep it steady.

She stood quickly, bottle in hand, and turned toward the kitchen.

But Danny's hand caught her arm—lightly, gently.

"Hey," he said, his eyes meeting hers. "Just—listen."

Her body froze.

He didn't grip her tight. Didn't pull. But the contact made her skin crawl.

"I really appreciate you letting me crash here," he said, his voice earnest. "And getting me the job at the Parrot? Even if all this is temporary, it's meant a lot. You've always had my back."

Pati's stomach bottomed out. Her smile returned, thinner this time. Like it was barely stitched together. "Oh. Yeah. Of course, Danny."

She didn't want to say his name.

She didn't want to say anything to him.

She didn't want to be touched, thanked, smiled at like they were sharing some sweet family moment. Not now. Not with everything she knew.

She needed him out of her house.

She stepped back, out of his reach, and his arm dropped limply into his lap. She turned to the kitchen and placed the bottle on the counter like it was radioactive. Her hands trembled as she unlocked her phone. She opened Nate's thread and typed two words: bottle found.

She hit send and slid the phone back into her pocket just as Danny spoke again.

"So…" he said casually, stretching his arms over his head, "what have you been up to this morning?"

Pati's mind stalled. *Oh, you know. Just calling the cops on you. Reconsidering every family memory we've ever shared. Learning you might be a delusional killer with a taste for French wine and women who look like my sister.*

She opened her mouth—but before she had to say anything, there was a knock at the door. Three sharp raps. Steady. Authoritative. Her heart stopped.

Danny raised an eyebrow. "You expecting someone?"

"Uh… yeah," she said quickly. "Plumber. Leak in the… you know. Pipes."

She moved toward the door like she was sleep-walking. Her hand gripped the knob a second too long before she finally pulled it open. Nate and Trent stood on her porch, both in plain clothes but wearing that unmistakable detective posture—shoulders squared, eyes already scanning the inside of her house over her shoulder.

"Morning," Trent said, expression unreadable.

Nate gave her the faintest nod.

"Hey," she whispered.

They stepped inside.

Danny, now fully sitting up on the couch, blinked at the two men. "Uh… can I help you?"

"Mr. Bishop?" Trent asked.

Danny glanced at Pati, then back. "Yeah. That's me."

Trent held up a badge. "Detective Morillo. This is Detective Rusiek. We just have a few questions for you. Mind if we sit?"

Danny's brows knitted together. "Uh… sure, I guess?"

Trent moved to the edge of the couch, seating himself in the nearby armchair, while Nate slipped past them and went straight for the kitchen counter—where the bottle of wine still sat.

Danny looked from one to the other, confused but not yet alarmed.

"What's this about?" he asked.

Trent opened a small notebook. "Do you remember what you did last night around 2 a.m.?"

Danny gave a short laugh. "I mean… not really. I had a few glasses of wine. Got into a bit of a dumb argument with Pati. Nothing major. Then I passed out on the couch. Why?"

Trent's eyes didn't leave him. "You didn't go out?"

"No." Danny frowned. "Why would I go out? I was wasted."

"You were drinking Beaujolais?"

Danny tilted his head. "Yeah. I think so. What's going on?"

While Trent kept the conversation going, Nate pulled a pair of gloves from his back pocket, snapped them on, and picked up the bottle of wine. He studied it briefly, then slipped it into an evidence bag, sealing it tight.

Danny's gaze flicked toward the kitchen. "Wait—what are you doing? Why are you bagging my wine?"

Trent kept his tone steady. "Mr. Bishop, you said you didn't leave the house last night. Is there anyone who can verify that?"

"Well, Pati was here."

Trent nodded slowly. "And where were you before you came home?"

Danny opened his mouth, but nothing came out.

"We're asking," Trent said carefully, "because a young woman was attacked last night near the Hogfish Bar. Around 2:30 in the morning. She described her assailant as barefoot, faking a French accent, and carrying a bottle of Beaujolais. You match the physical description."

Danny's eyes widened. "Wait—what? No. That—no. I didn't attack anyone. I don't even remember getting off the couch. Jesus Christ."

Nate stepped into the room now, quiet as a shadow, evidence bag in hand. Trent stood.

"Daniel Bishop," he said, "you are under arrest for the attempted assault of Rae Walker. You have the right to remain silent. Anything you say—"

"What the fuck?!" Danny shot up to his feet. "Are you serious? This is insane—I didn't do anything!"

Pati backed away, pulse thudding in her throat. She couldn't move. Couldn't speak.

Danny turned to her. "Pati, tell them! You know me! You know I wouldn't hurt anybody!"

But she couldn't meet his eyes. She just stared at the empty couch, the pillow still dented from where his head had been.

Trent and Nate flanked him quickly, pulling his hands behind his back. The cuffs clicked.

Danny didn't resist. He just kept shouting. "This is a

mistake! I didn't do anything! I swear to God—Pati!"

But Pati still didn't move. Because now that the tide had finally turned, she wasn't sure she could breathe. She watched as they took him away. And her house, for the first time in days, was quiet again. Too quiet.

CHAPTER 20
THE FARCE

For hours, Pati sat on the floor of her living room, legs sprawled out like a broken puppet, back against the wall. The couch—the one where Danny had been—loomed beside her like a crime scene that hadn't been taped off yet. The whole room smelled like salt, fabric softener, and stale wine.

At some point, she thought she passed out. Maybe. She couldn't be sure if it had been real sleep or one of those grief-numbed trances where your brain slips sideways and time stops making sense. Her limbs felt heavy, her throat dry. Her body ached in that peculiar way it does after crying just enough to be sore, but not enough to feel relief.

When she blinked awake again, the light in the room had shifted—tilted gold, like late afternoon. For a second, her mind played a cruel trick. She thought maybe it had all been a bad dream. Just one long, grotesque, poorly plotted nightmare.

She almost laughed. Almost. But then her eyes drifted toward the rug beneath her coffee table—her favorite throw rug, the one with the faded sunburst pattern and tiny tassels on each end—and there it was.

A red wine stain.

Faint, but unmistakable. The color of guilt and fingerprints.

No dream.

Her stomach twisted, and she curled forward, resting her head on her knees.

She hadn't moved since they'd taken Danny.

Nate had barely looked at her when they left. Not out of coldness—more like shellshock. Trent had nodded once, told her they'd be in touch. The door had closed behind them, and Pati hadn't stood up since.

Now, she forced herself upright with a groan, cracking every joint in the process. Her spine felt like it had been swapped for a stack of driftwood, brittle and uneven. She dragged herself to the kitchen and filled a glass with water from the tap, staring at it like it might offer answers. It didn't.

She pulled out her phone. Two texts.

One from Clara: *Taking off soon. Will keep you posted. Love you.*

And one from Nate: *We'll need to come back to search the place. Assume the knife he used to carve the wood is here somewhere. Will try to keep it low key. Let you know when.*

Pati dropped the phone on the counter like it burned. The idea of her home—her little safe, messy haven—being pawed through for evidence of a murder was too much. Or maybe it wasn't murder. Yet. Just attempted assault. The others still weren't officially connected. But she knew better. The driftwood carvings, the wine, the humming. "La Vie en Rose" like a ghost in the room.

Her whole body buzzed with a need to do something. Something stupid. Something predictable. She grabbed her keys and helmet and headed out the door.

The engine of the moped sputtered to life, and she gunned it harder than she meant to. The wind slapped her cheeks as she rode down the narrow street, eyes watering, the late sun low over the rooftops. It didn't take long.

The Green Parrot rose out of the palm trees like a temple of the familiar. Neon lights buzzing faintly, music bleeding out into the sidewalk, a smattering of locals on the benches out front, laughing too loud for the hour. She parked and walked in without even thinking.

The air inside was cool and dark, exactly how she liked it—how everyone liked it. A bubble of stillness in a too-bright world. The jukebox was silent for once, the pool table unoccupied. There were only a few people scattered at the bar, none of them familiar.

Except Rob. Rob was behind the bar, wiping down glasses, humming under his breath. He looked up when he saw her, and his face lit up with the kind of subtle relief that came from seeing someone you actually care about, even on the worst day.

"Hey, stranger," he said.

Pati didn't say anything for a beat. Then she slid onto a stool and exhaled for what felt like the first time all day.

"Hey," she croaked. "Thank God you're here."

Rob raised an eyebrow. "Rough morning?"

She gave a short, humorless laugh. "More like a rough… week. Month. Lifetime."

He didn't press. He knew what had been going on—just not how involved Pati's life had become. He grabbed a clean glass and poured her usual—neat, no questions asked. She took a sip and felt it warm all the way down, settling into the hollow ache behind her ribs.

"I heard something went down," Rob said gently.

"Something," she echoed. "Yeah, that's one way to put it."

He leaned on the counter across from her, towel slung over his shoulder. "You okay?"

"No."

There was no point lying.

He nodded like he got it. "Want to talk?"

She shook her head. "Not yet."

"Then drink," he said, sliding a napkin toward her like an offering. "And when you're ready… I'm here."

Pati closed her eyes and took another long sip.

She didn't want to talk. She wanted to forget. But sitting there, the jukebox still silent, Rob behind the bar like always, and the dull hum of island life carrying on outside, she knew forgetting wasn't possible.

Not anymore.

Not with blood in the sand.

Not with Danny's voice still echoing in her ears.

Not with her favorite rug stained in red.

Pati sat hunched over her drink, fingers curled loosely around the sweating glass. She wasn't drinking fast. She wasn't drinking slow. Just nursing it, like she needed the weight of it in her hand to remind her she still had a body. That she hadn't just dissolved into smoke after the week she'd had.

Locals trickled in, one by one, like clockwork. Regulars in tank tops and flip-flops and sunburned noses. Tourists wandered in early, wide-eyed and already too warm. And the stories. Oh, the stories were already flying.

She didn't even have to try to eavesdrop—they were everywhere. Floating between barstools, slipping down the tap line, bouncing off the warped wood paneling like echoes.

"Did you hear they got him?"

"Yeah, the guy who was pretending to be French."

"They say he was going after girls who looked like his ex-wife. Real creepy shit."

"Someone told me he carved stuff into driftwood. Like, messages. You believe that?"

"Frenchman my ass. Dude was probably from Jersey."

Pati stared down into her glass, letting the words swirl

around her like fog. She could feel the stories forming—already taking shape, mutating like folklore. Already, he was the Frenchman who wasn't a Frenchman. A myth. A punchline. A cautionary tale.

Undone by delusion.

Just a man who told himself a story one too many times and started believing it.

There was something almost tragic about it. Almost.

"Somebody said he was visiting family down here," one woman said two stools down. "That he just… snapped."

"No, no," a man replied. "He's a snowbird. One of those weird guys who comes down early and camps out. I swear I've seen him before—at the tiki bar near Smathers."

"Nah," said another. "He was living off the grid. That's why it took so long to catch him."

Theories spilled faster than the beer. Pati listened, quietly grateful that—for now—her name hadn't come up. No one mentioned her house. No one mentioned that the so-called Frenchman had been snoring on her couch, drinking from her glasses, bleeding wine onto her rug. She had Nate to thank for that.

She didn't know how he'd managed to keep it out of the gossip loop—maybe it was still coming—but for now, she could just be a girl at the bar. Another local drinking to forget.

Rob passed her again, and she gave him a grateful glance. He winked. No words. Just a soft knock of his knuckles against the bar. She was halfway through another sip when the bar phone rang.

Rob reached over, picked it up, and answered in his usual half-sung tone. "Parrot."

His brow lifted slightly. Then he turned to her.

"Pati," he said. "Call for you."

Her heart dropped. No one called the bar for her. No one even knew to. She blinked, confused, then slid off her stool and took the receiver from Rob's outstretched hand.

"Hello?"

The voice on the other end was unmistakable.

"Pati," said Michel, calm and deliberate. "I hope it wasn't someone you knew."

There was a pause. It hit her like a slow tide. Cold at first, then creeping over everything.

She swallowed.

"Michel," she said. "Where are you?"

"Palm Beach," he replied. "Continuing, what was it you called it—my tropical sabbatical?"

She could almost picture him, standing stiffly in a hotel hallway, one hand in his jacket pocket, chin lifted as if delivering a line from an old noir film.

"I saw the news," he said after a beat. "Or at least, the rumors. The man they're calling 'the Frenchman.' Quite a tale."

She pressed her fingers to her temple, rubbed the skin there like she could smooth out her own tension.

"Yeah," she said softly. "Quite a tale."

Another pause.

"Anyway," he continued, voice softening, "I just

wanted to say I'm glad it's over. For all of us. And I hope you're okay."

Pati closed her eyes. She wanted to say something—something that wrapped up the whole mess in a bow, or at least punched through the silence—but nothing came.

"I will be," she said.

She hung up before he could say anything else. She handed the phone back to Rob and returned to her seat, heart still thudding softly. I hope it wasn't someone you knew. But it was. That was the farce of it all. The story people told themselves to feel safe. It was never someone you knew. It was always the stranger. The shadow. The man in the mask.

But it was someone she knew. Someone who had bled into her life like spilled wine. And now the whole island was drinking the story down like rum.

She took another sip.

And let the farce carry on.

Pati's phone buzzed against the bartop. She didn't need to check it to know who it was.

She flipped it over anyway.

Clara: *Just landed.*

For a second, Pati didn't move. The words stared back at her like they'd time-traveled. A glitch in the matrix. Just landed—like this was some ordinary visit, like Clara was just flying in for the weekend, for brunch and beach days and an overdue sister catch-up. Instead, she was landing in the middle of a nightmare. Pati exhaled, rubbed her eyes, and typed back.

Pati: *Take a cab to the Green Parrot. I'm here.*

It took about thirty seconds for the dots to appear.

Clara: *Even with my luggage?*

Pati smirked despite herself. *Of course, Clara had brought real luggage.* Not a backpack, not a tote. Luggage. Zippers and compartments and airport tags and probably a travel steamer.

She tapped out a reply.

Pati: *Yes. We'll get someone to drive us back to my place.*

Another pause.

Clara: *Okay. See you soon.*

Pati slid the phone back onto the bar, upside down, wondering if they could even return to her place tonight. She stared at her drink for a moment longer, then pushed it away. She was already swimming in enough emotion—no need to add alcohol to the flood.

Clara was here. Really here. Pati turned in her seat, facing the doorway, waiting for the inevitable.

Twenty minutes later, the door creaked open and in walked Clara MacDonald Bishop—pristine as ever, even in 85 degrees and 80 percent humidity. Her dark hair was pulled into a low, tidy bun. She wore jeans, a loose white blouse, and flat sandals that somehow hadn't collected dust on the way from the cab. Her makeup was minimal but flawless. And yes, she was rolling a compact piece of navy blue luggage behind her like she was checking into a resort. She scanned the bar with surgical precision and spotted Pati instantly.

Pati waved. Clara didn't smile, but her shoulders relaxed just enough to be noticeable. As she walked over, the wheels of the suitcase thunked once against a cracked floor. Pati stood up to meet her. They didn't hug, not right away. Just stood there.

"I can't believe you brought a suitcase," Pati said finally, voice dry.

Clara arched her brow. "What was I supposed to do? Shove everything in a canvas bag like you?"

"Worked for me."

Clara exhaled a tired almost-laugh, then closed the last bit of distance between them and wrapped her arms around Pati. The hug was firm. Long. Not warm, exactly, but anchored. Like a hand clasped to a ledge after days in rough water. Pati hugged back and let herself lean into it. They separated after a moment, and Clara glanced around the bar.

"This is… atmospheric," she said.

"Don't judge the Parrot," Pati said. "It's held more of my breakdowns than any therapist ever has."

Clara gave a slow nod. "Fair."

Rob appeared behind the bar just in time to catch the tail end of the conversation.

"You must be Clara," he said, offering a hand across the bar.

Clara took it. "I am. And you are?"

"Rob. The only person keeping your sister hydrated." Pati snorted.

Clara managed a half-smile. "Well. Thanks for that."

Rob gave them both a nod and turned to refill someone's beer.

Pati gestured to the stool beside hers. "You want to sit? Or head out?"

Clara shook her head. "I think I've sat enough today. Let's go."

Clara looked at the barstool, then at the luggage still behind her, then back at Pati.

And to Pati's surprise, she sat.

"I need a drink," Clara said flatly, flagging Rob down with surprising efficiency.

Pati blinked. "Wait—you want a drink?"

Clara didn't even look at her. "Vodka cranberry. Tall. Light on the cranberry."

Rob arched a brow, already reaching for the vodka. "You got it."

Pati stared at her like she'd just announced she was getting a tattoo.

Clara turned, expression dry. "Don't look at me like that."

"I'm just… impressed," Pati said, amused. "Usually your idea of cutting loose is ordering a decaf after 6 p.m."

"I'm evolving," Clara replied, grabbing a cocktail napkin and laying it down neatly in front of her. "Trauma'll do that."

Pati laughed—a real, surprised laugh—and for the first time in what felt like days, something inside her unclenched. Rob placed the drink in front of Clara and gave them a little salute before disappearing down the bar again.

Clara took a sip and nodded approvingly. "Not bad."

"Welcome to the dark side," Pati said, raising her glass.

They clinked. And then, for a moment, the silence between them wasn't tense or awkward or full of unspoken guilt. It was just quiet. Comfortable. Familiar.

CHAPTER 21
SISTERS REUNITED

Pati leaned back against the bar. "Remember that one time you had half a glass of sangria at Mom's retirement party and cried for like an hour about her getting old?"

"She is getting old," Clara said, faux-defensive.

"You also told me—verbatim—that your soul was wilting like an unloved fern."

Clara groaned. "Oh God. That's embarrassing."

Pati grinned. "It's my favorite quote from you of all time."

Clara sipped her drink and gave a dramatic sigh. "Well, brace yourself, because my soul is still a little wilted. But this"—she gestured toward the bar—"is helping."

"See?" Pati said. "Told you the Parrot heals."

They fell into easy conversation, surprisingly so. There were still shadows at the edges—of course there were—but for the first time in years, they were just talking. No measuring. No skirting. Just sisters. Mid-drink. Mid-mess. Mid-something that felt like real connection.

"I really am sorry," Pati said after a while, voice

lower. "For not calling more. For… not seeing what he was doing to you."

Clara was quiet for a beat. Then she nodded. "I'm sorry too. I should've asked for help sooner. But I was embarrassed. And angry. And… I didn't want to believe it was what it was."

"I get it," Pati said. "We always made excuses for the men in our lives. Mom did it. Nana did it. Guess we both inherited that habit."

Clara swirled the ice in her drink. "Yeah. Well. Consider me in recovery."

Pati grinned. "Cheers to that."

They toasted again.

Rob came by and slid a fresh napkin under Clara's nearly empty glass. "Another?"

Clara glanced at Pati. Then shrugged.

"One more," she said. "I'm off the clock."

Pati raised her glass again. "I cannot believe you just said that."

"What? I can be fun!"

"No one's denying that," Pati said. "It's just… like spotting a unicorn. In a business-casual blazer."

Clara gave her a look. "I hate you."

"No, you don't."

"No," Clara agreed, softening. "I really don't."

They both looked down at their drinks then, smiling faintly. For the first time in a long time, Pati felt the ache of what had been missing between them—and the quiet relief of having it begin to return. Maybe, after all the damage and all the silence and all the years they'd spent standing just a little too far apart, they were finally finding their way back. One drink at a time.

Pati didn't hear her phone buzz the first time.

Or the second.

Or the third.

She was too deep in the moment—half-laughing, half-listening as Clara recounted a bizarre work retreat that involved a ropes course, a collapsed teepee, and someone named Gary getting stung by a jellyfish because he wanted to "test the tides."

"I told him not to swim after tacos," Clara said, rolling her eyes. "But nooo, Gary knew his body."

Pati wheezed. "God, I forgot how dumb corporate people can be."

"Some of them," Clara said. "Others just quietly drink and wait for Gary to fail. I've chosen the latter."

They clinked their glasses again, only ice and cranberry juice left in Clara's by now, and Pati felt something flutter in her chest. It wasn't joy exactly, but it was close— maybe something older, buried under years of guilt and silence. Something like sisterhood.

Then a shadow appeared in her periphery.

A familiar one.

Nate.

He stepped in from the doorway, scanning the bar until his eyes landed on her. His jaw was set, and his shoulders were tight, like he'd been holding in bad news for miles. Pati's stomach dropped. She reached for her phone instinctively and found four unread texts from him.

Where are you?

Need to talk.

Can't reach you.

Parrot?

She slid off the stool as Nate approached, a wave of guilt washing over her.

"Hey," she said. "Sorry, I didn't see—"

"It's okay," Nate interrupted, though his voice was tight. "I figured this might be where you'd be."

Clara stood beside her, posture straightening into something unreadable. Professional. Guarded. Nate's eyes flicked to her, then back to Pati.

"Can we talk?"

Pati's gut twisted. "Here's fine. What's going on?"

Nate sighed. "Just came from your place. Morillo and forensics are still inside. They've found a few items of interest, including what we think is the carving knife. But the house is still an active scene."

"I thought you were going to tell me before going over there?"

"Well it's not like I didn't try," Nate gave Pati a stern look.

Clara's eyebrows lifted. "Okay so we knew you'd find those things. What does that mean for us?"

"Sorry, who are you?" Nate stopped, looking quizzically between Pati and Clara.

"What? You don't see the family resemblance?" Pati quipped.

Nate blinked. "This is your sister?"

"Hi, Clara MacDonald Bishop," Clara extended her hand. "Well probably just Clara MacDonald again now."

Nate shook her hand. "I wouldn't blame you." He cracked a smile. "So about your place."

"Oh no," Pati said. "What is it?"

"You're not allowed to return there tonight. It's honestly probably going to be about a week."

Pati's heart sank.

"I get it," she said. "But… where are we supposed to go?"

"The department's willing to put you up in a hotel," Nate said. "If you want. On the city's tab."

Clara turned to her. "That's not… the worst thing."

"No," Pati admitted. "It's just… weird."

"Weird how?" Nate asked.

"Having strangers comb through my underwear drawer, mostly."

Nate gave her a small, sympathetic smile, but the exhaustion in his face lingered.

"I know it sucks," he said. "But it's protocol."

Clara nodded tightly, then looked to Pati. "Well. I guess we'll go pack a bag and—oh. Right. No bags. No access."

"We can swing by tomorrow," Nate said. "I'll clear it. You'll be able to grab a few essentials, then we'll keep the place closed until forensics is done."

Pati rubbed her temples. "Great. Guess it's a hotel mini shampoo kind of night."

They stood there in an awkward triangle—Pati with her arm crossed, Clara pulling out her phone to look up hotels, Nate waiting like he didn't want to leave but didn't know what to say next. And then—

"Well, shit."

All three heads turned. An older woman in a sleeveless button-down, neon coral lipstick, and a wide-brimmed sunhat sauntered up to the bar like she owned it—which, in some ways, she kind of did.

"Betty?" Pati blinked.

"You can stay with me," Betty said. "I'll even charge ya if the Key West PD is footing the bill."

Pati's jaw dropped, then curved into a grateful, stunned grin. Betty winked.

"I came lookin' for you when I heard they arrested someone down by Hogfish," she said, plopping herself onto the stool Pati had vacated. "That's your neck of the woods, so I figured I'd check in. And wouldn't you know it? Found you at the Parrot."

She pulled a fan from her purse and started waving it gently, like it was just another Monday. Pati moved toward her, torn between laughing and hugging her.

"I… wow. Thank you. I don't even know what to say.

I really have no idea how to explain what's happened ."

"Don't say anything yet," Betty replied, waving a dismissive hand. "We'll get some bourbon in me and then you can start explaining things. Or don't. But this isn't the time or the place. The walls have ears on most of this island."

Clara stepped closer, politely but visibly unsure what to make of the woman with glittery flip-flops and a parrot earring in one ear. Betty looked her over.

"You haven't introduced me to the new girl," she said, still fanning herself. "I take it this must be your sister?"

Clara extended her hand. "Clara MacDonald."

"Betty Martinez," she said, shaking it firmly. "Don't let the old-lady exterior fool you. I can outdrink most of the men in this bar and still be up for sunrise yoga."

Clara blinked, then smiled. "I think I like you already."

"Good. I'm like fungus," Betty said. "I grow on people. Whether they want me to or not."

Nate cleared his throat, but there was a slight smile tugging at the corners of his mouth. "I'll, uh, let the department know you two have a place to stay."

"Damn right they do," Betty said. "And you can bill them for the air conditioning I'm gonna crank to arctic, too."

Pati couldn't help it—she laughed. A real, deep, full-body laugh.

Relief.

Gratitude.

And the absurdity of it all.

Betty stood and patted her on the arm. "Finish your

drink. We'll swing by my place after. You're not the first woman I've sheltered after a breakdown, and you sure as hell won't be the last."

Pati turned to Clara, who looked equally bemused and relieved.

"Guess we're not going to a hotel," Pati said.

"Guess not," Clara echoed.

Betty had already turned to the bar, ordering a whiskey neat like the day hadn't even happened.

And maybe that was the best part. The world was still spinning. The bar was still open. The stories were still being told. But for the first time in days, Pati didn't feel like she was spinning out with it.

She had a place to go.

She had her sister beside her.

And she had Betty—blunt, strange, brilliant Betty—making room for her in the storm.

CHAPTER 22
CAN'T ESCAPE THE MOON

The back bungalow behind Betty's house was smaller than Pati remembered. She'd crashed there once before, a few years back, after a particularly disastrous breakup and a rum-soaked night that ended in karaoke and crying. Back then, it had felt like exile. Tonight, it felt like a soft landing.

She and Clara stood just inside the door, bags in hand, taking it in. The place smelled faintly of coconut lotion and cedar. A small twin window unit buzzed from the corner, humming a lullaby of comfort. The floor creaked, but the walls were solid. There was a double bed and a dresser painted a faded turquoise. A string of seashells hung in the window like a curtain fringe.

Clara looked like she'd just been assigned a bunk at summer camp.

"Well," she said, tilting her head, "it's… charming."

Pati snorted. "Admit it. You're uncomfortable. No hotel minibar, no turn-down service, no complimentary slippers."

Clara side-eyed her. "I do like a good robe."

"Oh my God, you're such a city girl."

"And you," Clara said, dropping her bag onto the bed closest to the dresser, "have officially become one of those fruitcakes who lives in Key West and collects decorative sea glass."

Pati beamed. "That might be the nicest thing you've ever said to me."

They both laughed, and for a moment it was just easy. Sisters. Talking shit. No killer. No headlines. No wine-stained rugs or shattered trust. Just two women sharing the air again.

Clara started unpacking immediately, because of course she did. Pati watched as her sister hung up a button-down blouse and two neatly folded cardigans. She wasn't even going to be here more than a couple days, and already she was settling in like she planned to host a TED Talk.

Pati sat on the edge of the bed and toed off her shoes. Her whole body ached—not from any single injury but from the sheer weight of the last ten days. From the moment she first heard about the murders to the moment they led Danny away in cuffs. It lived in her bones now.

"I'm gonna shower," she said, standing with a stretch.

Clara nodded. "There are fresh towels in the cabinet by the door. Betty told me."

"Noted."

Pati grabbed her overnight bag and disappeared into the tiny bathroom, letting the door close behind her. She peeled off her clothes, turned the water as hot as she could stand it, and stepped in. The water hit her like a wave.

It wasn't just about being clean. It was about shedding something. She closed her eyes and let it run over her face, her scalp, her shoulders—like she could rinse the last week off her skin and send it spiraling down the drain. The fear. The doubt. The strange guilt she carried in her chest like a bruise. She stayed until the mirror fogged and her fingers wrinkled. When she came out wrapped in a towel, the lights were off and Clara was already tucked in bed on the far side of the room.

The soft blue glow of the moon peeked in through the sheer curtain, casting a gentle wash over everything. Pati could just make out the shape of her sister's back beneath the perfectly aligned sheets. Her suitcase had been slid under the bed. Probably empty now, its contents organized in drawers Pati hadn't even looked at.

Very Clara.

Pati smiled softly in the dark.

She dropped the towel, pulled on a loose tank top and shorts, and climbed into the other bed—close enough to feel the presence of someone else, but not touching. The ceiling fan spun above them in slow circles, stirring the air just enough to make the sheet feel like safety instead of a net.

She missed her bed. Missed her apartment. Missed her pillow that smelled like sun and salt. But she didn't miss being alone. She watched the fan for a while, her thoughts like bubbles rising slowly to the surface. The night was still happening somewhere outside.

Cops at her house.

Reporters sniffing around.

A town already rewriting the story.

But here, in the soft dark of the bungalow, her sister breathing slowly and evenly beside her, Pati felt—for the first time in days—something close to peace.

It wouldn't last.

It never did.

But she would take it.

And tomorrow?

Tomorrow could be messy.

Tonight, the moonlight was enough.

A few days later, Pati sat on the porch swing beside Clara, both of them barefoot, each with a sweating glass of something cool and citrusy in hand. The sun had dipped below the horizon, painting the sky in shades of mango and coral. A soft breeze stirred the palm fronds. Crickets had started their nightly chorus, and from somewhere down the street came the faint sound of a conga drum, like a heartbeat pulsing through the island. Betty sat across from them in her favorite wicker chair, one leg crossed over the other, fan lazily drifting in front of her face.

It had been a few days since Danny's arrest. And while the air still felt thick with the aftermath, it was no longer unbearable.

"Y'all are lucky," Betty said, sipping from her own glass. "You got a good porch tonight. No bugs, no downpour. Just stars and secrets."

"Sounds like a romance novel," Pati said.

Betty winked. "Don't tempt me. I've got a half-written one in my drawer."

They all chuckled, the kind of low, genuine laughter that comes when the tension has eased just enough to allow it.

"I was thinking about Casey earlier," Pati said, after a moment of silence.

Clara turned to her. "Casey?"

"Yeah," Pati nodded. "A friend of mine. She moved down here from Cincinnati. Quit her corporate job. Just… left. Didn't even have a plan. She was supposed to stay for a few weeks, get her head on straight."

"And?" Clara asked.

"She met this sexy French tattoo artist and now lives with him," Pati said, grinning. "Last I saw her, she was barefoot, suntanned, and wildly in love. Pretty sure she hasn't worn a blazer in at least six months."

Clara laughed. "God, that sounds like a fever dream."

"Right?" Pati leaned back. "She actually lived in this bungalow before us. Betty rented it to her when she first landed."

"She was a sweet one," Betty added. "Used to leave handpicked hibiscus in a jar on my porch every Sunday morning. Like clockwork."

"I don't think I've ever even seen a hibiscus," Clara said.

"See? You really are a city girl," Pati teased, bumping Clara's knee gently with her own.

Clara rolled her eyes, but her smile lingered. "Look, I'll give you this. The island's charming. But I couldn't stay here. My job wouldn't allow it. I've got a whole life up in Tennessee. Friends. A dentist I trust. And to be perfectly honest, I think I've had enough of the word 'Frenchman' to last a lifetime, so I'm good on the sexy French tattoo artists."

Betty cackled. "That's what they all say."

"But seriously," Clara continued, her voice softening, "I do need to stick around long enough to clear up everything. Danny's mess… it left a trail."

Betty's face shifted—less amused, more grounded. "What's the update on that?"

Pati sighed. "Well, they found the knife he used to carve the driftwood. It had his fingerprints. And they've got his DNA. Matches what they pulled off the scene behind Hogfish. It's airtight."

Clara looked down at her drink. Her fingers were still, but her jaw was clenched.

"He picked those women," she said. "Because they looked like me."

"Clara—" Pati started.

"I know I didn't tell him to do it," she said quickly. "I know it's not my fault. But I can't stop thinking—what if I'd gotten out sooner? What if I'd filed that police report years ago? Or taken his meds to the authorities? Or told you the truth and asked for help sooner?"

Betty shook her head. "Honey, you can 'what if' yourself into the grave. Doesn't mean any of it's your fault."

"You were surviving," Pati added, more gently now. "You were doing what you had to do. And you did get out. That matters."

Clara looked at her, eyes glassy. "It just… doesn't feel like enough."

"It never does," Betty said. "Not when love gets tangled up in the damage."

Clara swallowed hard. "I didn't just lose a partner. I lost the version of myself that thought I was safe."

No one said anything for a moment. The crickets filled in the silence.

Finally, Betty straightened a little. "Well. You're both welcome to stay here as long as you need. But fair warning—I do charge for the bungalow once the police department stops footing the bill and Pati gets back home."

That got a laugh out of Clara.

"Understood," she said. "I'll keep the tab open."

Pati smiled. "We'll leave you a hibiscus in a jar."

Betty raised her glass. "Make it two."

They sipped in companionable silence again, the

moon rising high over the porch now, bright and round and impossible to ignore.

"So what's next?" Betty asked. "Trial? Bail hearing?"

"Nate says Danny's lawyer is going for an insanity plea," Pati said. "They've already started building the case. His diagnosis, history, breakdowns—all of it."

Clara let out a soft exhale. "Which… isn't totally untrue. He is sick. He does need help."

"Help doesn't mean forgiveness," Betty said.

"I know," Clara replied. "But I keep thinking—if someone had stepped in years ago, maybe none of this would've happened."

"You stepped in now," Pati said. "You told the truth. That matters."

"They might plead it down," Clara said. "Reduced sentence. State hospital. Something like that."

Betty tilted her head. "Insanity pleas don't usually stick. Judges don't like mysteries."

Pati raised an eyebrow. "Is there something you're not telling us? Are you a crime expert now, Betty?"

Betty grinned. "Listen—I've watched a documentary or two."

Clara laughed. "Any of those documentaries tell you why they did it?"

Betty leaned back, gaze drifting skyward. The fan in her hand paused mid-air.

"Oh, honey," she said. "You can blame it on the Champs-Élysées, or you can blame it on a tune. Hell, you can blame it on the stroke of Monet." She looked at them then—steady, clear-eyed. "But you can't escape the moon."

The words sat between them, soft and haunting. Pati stared out past the porch railing, watching the moon cast silver on the tops of the palms. She didn't know if Betty was right. She didn't know if anyone could really explain the kind of madness Danny had fallen into. But somehow, the line felt true. There were things that pulled at people. Things that changed them. And maybe the moon had always had something to do with it.

EPILOGUE

It had been just over a week since Pati and Clara had settled into Betty's back bungalow, and though the salt air still felt a little heavier than usual and the headlines hadn't fully faded, something had shifted. The door to the porch creaked open, and Nate stepped in like he'd done it a hundred times before—casual, sun-kissed, and carrying that same clipboard he always claimed he didn't need.

"Morning," he said, offering a small smile.

Pati looked up from her iced coffee. "Hey. You lost or just trying to avoid paperwork again?"

"Neither," he said, pulling a folded paper from his back pocket. "I come bearing good news. You're officially cleared to move back in."

Her eyebrows rose. "Seriously?"

He nodded. "Forensics wrapped yesterday. We tried to keep it as clean as we could. They were careful. But… you know. It's still gonna feel off. Might want to give the place a refresh."

She took the paper from his hand and studied it like it might dissolve. The word Released in the top corner made her breath catch.

"Thanks, Nate," she said, more quietly now.

He shrugged. "If you want to repaint the whole place for a fresh start, I'm in. I've got some days off coming up. We'll make it look brand new."

Pati smiled, touched by the offer. "That's kind of you."

He looked over her shoulder toward the bungalow and added, "Seriously. Anything you need."

She nodded, and after a moment, turned toward the porch door.

"Betty!" she called. "I'm gonna be heading out in a few days. Just need to get the place aired out and cleaned up first."

Betty emerged from inside, wiping her hands on a dish towel like some sitcom landlady. "Well, I'll miss your face," she said, then turned her attention to Clara. "What about you? Heading back to your big-city glass tower or sticking around to become another Key West legend?"

Clara glanced up from her book, her legs tucked under her in one of Betty's worn chairs. "I've got a few things left to wrap up with the police. And I can't just leave Pati hanging. Someone's gotta help put that place back together. I still feel like I opened the damn door that let Danny slither down here in the first place."

Pati didn't even wait. "Clara. You didn't. We've been over this."

"I know," Clara said softly. "But still. I want to help."

"I'm not stopping you," Pati replied with a grin. "We've got walls to repaint."

"I've got primer in the shed," Betty said. "And wine in

the fridge. I know my role."

Nate looked at Clara with an easy wink. "Well, good. It'll be nice seeing you around town a little longer."

Clara gave him a smile that was part amused, part curious. "That right?"

He nodded. "Absolutely."

The sun was sinking behind the palm trees, throwing long shadows over the yard, but the air still held its warmth. A rooster called somewhere in the distance, and the breeze carried the scent of salt.

For a moment, it was just quiet. Not the kind of silence that used to haunt Pati in the middle of the night, but something steadier. Like breath. Like beginning.

She looked out toward the street, past the fence, toward the direction of home. It didn't feel cursed anymore. It felt ready. And maybe that's what healing really was—not forgetting, not undoing, but choosing to walk through the wreckage anyway, paintbrush in one hand and your sister at your side.

The ghosts of the island would never truly leave. They lived in the shadows, in the wind, in the clink of bottles at the bars around town. But so did love. And on this island, it was sometimes hard to tell the difference.

ABOUT THE AUTHOR

H.R. Gordon is a writer, publisher, and lifelong beach bum at heart. The founder of Gordon Publishing and the imprint Beach Bum Books, Hannah brings to life stories soaked in sunshine, sea breeze, and second chances. With a career spanning more than a decade in publishing—as a copywriter, editor, marketer, and acquisitions manager—she knows her way around a good story and how to bring it into the world.

When she's not writing novels set in salty, sun-drenched places, Hannah is likely listening to Jimmy Buffett with a tropical drink in hand, dreaming up her next island escape. Her deep love for Key West—its music, magic, and motley cast of characters—inspires every page she writes.

Hannah lives in Buffalo, New York, with her librarian partner and three dogs, but her heart is always somewhere south of the mainland. Whether she's working on the next Beach Bum Book manuscript or diving into one of her many creative projects, she's here to prove that paradise is more than a place—it's a state of mind.

ABOUT THE SERIES

The BEACH BUM BOOKS romance and mystery series are sister series' set in the same sun-drenched universe—where dive bars, boat docks, and buried secrets collide. Each book can be read on its own, but keep an eye out for familiar faces and favorite hangouts popping up across stories.

Fall in love with a Key West romance one day, then dive into a tropical whodunit the next. If you find yourself missing a character, don't worry—they might just wander into the next Beach Bum book, cocktail in hand. You never quite know who you'll run into on the island.

ABOUT THE PUBLISHER

BEACH BUM BOOKS is your ultimate destination for sun-soaked stories and tropical tales. We're all about the laid-back, beach bum lifestyle, bringing you captivating reads that whisk you away to sandy shores and sunny skies.

Whether you're lounging by the ocean, dreaming of your next seaside escape, or simply looking for a moment of paradise in your day, we've got you covered. Plus, a portion of proceeds from all Beach Bum Books sales supports Save the Manatee, Mr. Jimmy Buffett's nonprofit organization.

So, grab your favorite beach chair, sip a tropical drink, and get ready to escape with Beach Bum Books—where every page is a step closer to paradise.